S.A. MOSSMAN

The Tree of Life

Daedalus Detective Story #1

First published by Under A Neon Sky Publishing 2023

Copyright © 2023 by S.A. Mossman

This novel is entirely a work of fiction. The names, characters and incidents portrayed in it are the work of the author's imagination. Any resemblance to actual persons, living or dead, events or localities is entirely coincidental.

First edition

ISBN: 979-8-9878529-0-3

This book was professionally typeset on Reedsy.
Find out more at reedsy.com

Dedicated to those of us still haunted by the past.

Contents

Daedalus & Icarus

Prologue

The witching hour gave way to a misty night cast under a full moon, illuminating quiet city streets, where the starlight was absent save twinkling bulbs glowing through open windows scattered across the skyline. The city was busy 24/7. Always packed and bustling with bodies maneuvering the complex labyrinth. Finding their night's adventure. Finding their next dream to chase. Everywhere was energy. Except the city's dock. The boats and barges sat empty and alone. In its late-night absence of life came the gentle lapping of water cresting in waves, the moon pushing and pulling against the sea, moving against the pier. The creeks of old wood. The salty night air. In the cold, voices carried. A slight, whispered word answered before it faded and returned to silence. The sounds of scuffling, the movements of something heavy. Silence. Muffled voices through concrete walls. Car doors opening. Closing. An engine starts and tires pull away. The gentle music of water lapping against the shore.

In a sudden burst of flames, the quiet was torn asunder. Fire spilled into the night sky blooming through the loud crash of concrete and wood suddenly exploding. The world came to life in the uproar. Sounds of screaming rang out as the fire

1

raged, seizing everything around it.

In a car a mile away, a man sat in the back seat, clothes disheveled, seat belt unbuckled. The few cars around them had stopped, their passengers standing outside their vehicles staring back at the unfurling chaos. The man kept looking forward, the car politely navigating the frozen vehicles. Dancing lights from police cars cruising by tinted the streets blue then red, over and over. He gripped a bag in his lap tight, his other hand resting on another, pulling it closer against him. He quietly watched the two men in front. Neither spoke. They cut large and imposing shadows under street lamps, red and blue illuminating broad faces till the cop cars passed leaving them in shadow again. They continued down the street, turning casually around a corner, disappearing into the heart of the city.

Chapter One

The city seemed scarcely awake as the sun drifted in over a milky fog permeating the skyline, cutting across the gaps between buildings, and filling the roadways. Slowly people trickled out of buildings, till the streams became steady, and along with them, cars and the beginning strains of the day drifting up above the city. Sadie stood tired and watching with dark bleary eyes. The night before had stretched into the day turning inky skies red. She had watched the sunrise from here, looking out the window of her latest client's high-rise apartment, standing among expensive furniture in her old leather jacket, heavy boots treading across hardwood floors, and looking out floor-to-ceiling windows at the city below while her client Anna made coffee in the next room. It seemed absurd given the nature of this early morning visit, but she'd learned that hiding in the little things gave people comfort when everything was about to be upended. If everything's normal maybe the hurt won't seep in. But it always finds its way in. Through all the little cracks in your armor.

Anna returned carrying two mugs of coffee, her eyes already rimmed red. Sadie took the steaming mug offered to her, grateful for the warmth pouring through the ceramic. She handed Anna the file folder she had brought along containing all the details of this case. Anna gave a reflexive smile, subtle wrinkles crinkling the corners of her warm eyes. The smile passed quickly, Anna's face turning dour as she stared at the cream-colored envelope.

"Thank you, Miss Park," Anna said, nodding slightly. "This will really help with the divorce proceedings." She sat on the nearby sofa placing the cup and the folder on the coffee table. She reached for her purse absently. Sadie sipped the coffee hoping it would wake her up long enough to drag herself home. Digging through her bag Anna produced a checkbook and pen. Hurriedly she scribbled on one of its pages and with a sniffle tore it from the book extending it towards Sadie. Sadie plucked the paper from her hand gently. "I'd cash that as soon as possible." Sadie nodded, tucking the check in her pocket.

"Are you gonna be okay?" Sadie asked, eyes searching the woman. She looked tired, like everything in her had drained away.

"No." She sniffled again, wiping away at her eyes with the back of her hand. "Probably not for a while," she sighed.

"If you need anything else..." Sadie said, drifting off before setting the coffee cup down on the table.

"I'll tell you," Anna said. "I think I want to be alone now." She stood to see Sadie out.

"I can see myself out," Sadie said, walking to the apartment door. Before letting herself out she turned back towards the other woman, "I'm sorry, Anna." Then she left her alone with the fallout.

The apartment hallway was ghostly quiet. She was thankful for the peace. Sadie hated the fraught emotions that came with her cases. She didn't know anything about Anna other than she seemed nice and probably didn't deserve her husband cheating on her. The elevator ride to the lobby gave her tired mind time to clear, the caffeine slowly taking hold of her foggy brain. The elevator doors slid open revealing the lobby's marble floor, its crystal chandelier twinkling in the morning sunlight. The city street beyond was already flooded with noise, every inch crawling with people and cars rushing around. Sadie took a deep breath and slipped into the stream, keeping pace with the crowd, constantly thinking of where to go. She needed to cash that check before Anna's husband cleared their bank out or whatever Anna thought might happen. Reaching into her jacket pocket she found a cell phone but no wallet. Patting herself down didn't yield any results.

"Damn it!" She stopped in the flow of foot traffic passerbys giving her dirty looks as they passed. Thinking frantically Sadie realized the offending items must be in her office. She could get it, take a nap and cash her check. Then finally call this long day over.

With her new destination in mind, she began navigating the city streets finding the nearest subway entrance. Like everything else, the subway car was filled to bursting with people only beginning their day. Sadie found a place to stand grasping onto a railing, tucking her free hand in her jacket pocket. She watched the passengers come and go as the car lurched forward and came to sudden stops, her tired mind blending the faces together till a woman with warm auburn hair passed by, and while she couldn't quite catch her face, she felt something so familiar that it froze her in place, made her heart race against her ribcage till she thought she might stop breathing. The woman found a seat, turning so Sadie could finally see her face. No. It wasn't her. Her heart slowly returned to normal. She was tired. That was all. The train sped to its next stop halting at the platform. The car felt too suffocating. She slid out the doorway just as the doors opened, deciding to walk the rest of the way.

She breathed the fresh air greedily feeling a little more awake. Sadie knew the streets so well that she scarcely had to think where to go. A small blessing in her current state. One of the few perks of growing up in the city. You knew your way around even the shittiest parts. Her phone started ringing in her pocket. The phone screen illuminated with the name 'Hector Reyes'.

"Hector!" Sadie said into the speaker.

"Sadie! How are you?" Hector asked. The familiar voice warmed her. Hector was like a parent to her. Along with his wife Marissa. Together they had looked out for Sadie when her own parents had been too drunk and absent to do it. They were private investigators and they taught Sadie everything she knew about the trade.

"I've been better," Sadie said. "Wrapping up an all-nighter. On my way back to the office as we speak."

"How's everything with Daedalus?" Hector asked.

"Business has been good. Thankfully," she said, moving on autopilot around clusters of people on the populated sidewalks, dodging broken parts of the cement. "How's retired life?"

"Did you hear about the explosion last night?" Hector ignored her question, excitedly asking one of his own instead. Sadie could envision his raised eyebrows, the glint of excitement in his dark eyes when there were unanswered questions.

"I was working. I caught a little on a diner tv earlier." From where Sadie stood she could begin to make out the building that housed her detective agency.

"Look into it after you get some rest," Hector said. "It's national news. Are you excited?"

"What?" Sadie said approaching the building, fishing a set of keys from her pocket. At least she hadn't misplaced those.

"Its been a year since you've taken over Daedalus. That's something to be proud of," Hector said, clearly plenty proud for her.

"I think we're a few days off from one year," Sadie sighed, absently unlocking the front door. Neglecting the mail piling high on the ground, she climbed the stairs as fast as she could, fighting her weary state. At the top of the stairs was the door for Daedalus Detective Agency, the business Sadie had inherited from the Reyes'.

"Marissa says hello, and she misses you," Hector continued in Sadie's ear. She wasn't paying much attention. Standing outside the office door was a woman with auburn hair casually waiting. She noticed Sadie right away, her face flush with recognition and relief.

"H-hector, I have to go," Sadie said, hanging up the phone before she could hear Hector's farewell. Sadie's mind was painfully blank as her heart did that awful lurch.

"Sadie?" the woman said, her voice hesitant. She looked more beautiful than Sadie remembered, her warm hair spilling down to her shoulders, her eyes soulful and currently scanning Sadie for some kind of reaction.

"Kat?" Sadie asked. "Did you take the subway here?" she continued in her overtired haze.

"N-no. A cab," Kat answered.

Good.

"Well, at least I'm not going crazy," Sadie sighed. Kat only stared at her, eyes bewildered. She looked on the verge of tears. Sadie thought she might be sick. Her mind unfurled into an overrun mess of memories. Tangles of memories from a lifetime ago. Her exhausted brain summoned images of childhood, every waking moment spent with Kat, every moment Kat gave her that cautious smile like the one she was wearing now.

"You know," Kat began, taking a small step toward Sadie. "Sometimes I think I see you. Just out in a crowd, or in a random car on the road, and I nearly have a heart attack. Now that you're right here. It's surreal." Her eyebrows raised, eyes still searching Sadie "Can we go inside?"

Sadie nodded. She steadied herself for a moment before moving past Kat to open the office door, feeling her eyes on her the entire time. She had spent ten years thinking about what an encounter like this might be like and now it was at her doorstep and the only thought materializing was *why?* With a turn of the key, the door opened and with a sweeping gesture she ushered Kat in. The other woman moved past her, shoulders brushing as she passed.

"I haven't been here since we were 17," Kat said, approaching the solitary office desk in the heart of the room. Sadie shut the door behind them. Kat was leaning against her desk, cast in the morning sunlight flooding through the windows. She looked so different from the girl she knew. More herself somehow. Sadie stood before her, the same question running through her head.

"What are you doing here?"

"I need your help," Kat said earnestly, straight to the point, meeting Sadie eye to eye. She could hear the creeping sadness in her voice.

"Of course. You wouldn't come here to see me." Sadie felt the long-suppressed anger biting into her, seeping out despite herself.

"After everything? I'm probably the last person you want to see." Kat kept watching her, her voice playfully warm and self-deprecating.

"That isn't true," Sadie said. Kat's face turned serious, the playfulness trickling away. "How'd you know where to find me?"

"I just figured," Kat said, scanning the office, fidgeting under Sadie's gaze. "Place hasn't changed much."

"Not much reason to," Sadie answered, stepping closer till she was seated on the desk next to Kat, hands pressed into the desk on either side of her. "What do you need?"

Kat met her gaze suddenly, her face painfully close to Sadie's now. Something heavy floated in the air between them. Kat swallowed hard, her eyebrows furrowing. Sadie gripped the edge of the desk harder. After a moment Kat answered.

"I came here right from the airport. I received a phone call. Two days ago," Kat drifted off, suddenly staring at Sadie's clenched hands. Glancing up to meet her eyes she continued. "It was my dad."

"You haven't heard from him since you were-"

"10," Kat finished for her.

"What'd he want?" Sadie asked, remembering the man she had known in her childhood. His charm and wit, his infrequent presence in her friend's life.

"$80,000 dollars. At first," Kat said.

"Ouch," Sadie replied. "I'm not terribly surprised."

"Neither was I," Kat continued. "I didn't have it anyway. He said not to worry, then he hung up. He called back a day ago. He gave me a name to look up and said he didn't know what was going to happen. That he loved me…" Kat trailed off.

"What was the name?" Sadie asked, voice low in the quiet of the office.

"Some woman in the midwest," Kat answered. "He wasn't there though. The phone number he called from, it's for a bar not far from here. I called. The bartender said he lives close by. She gave me the building name."

"You want to find your dad and what? Bail him out of whatever mess he's made?" Sadie asked.

"I just want to know he's okay," Kat said. "I don't think I can help him." She sighed. "I don't think anyone could help." Reaching into her purse she produced a slip of paper. She passed it to Sadie. A check, written out in her neat handwriting.

"I don't want your girlfriend's money," Sadie said, handing it back to her. Kat refused it.

"Please," Kat said, her hand resting on Sadie's outstretched hand, the check still in her grasp. Sadie's stomach fluttered at the contact. "I need you. You're the only person I trust in this city."

Sadie nodded.

"Okay." She ran a hand through her hair. "I'll start today."

"Good." Kat smiled at her, hand still on Sadie's, working whatever magic she possessed. "We can go to his apartment right now."

"What?" Sadie asked, pulling her hand away from Kat's. "I'll help you, but only on my own."

"I just thought-"

"Look," Sadie said, standing to face Kat. "You just show up asking for help, throwing money at me. It's been ten years. You were my best friend," Sadie's voice broke. Kat's eyes grew wide. She looked away from Sadie, "The last time I saw you we made love, and then you moved across the country with your fucking girlfriend. What do you want from me?"

Kat stood approaching Sadie. Resting one hand on her shoulder. "I don't expect you to forgive me for my bullshit. I don't forgive me. I think about it every day. I wonder if you're doing okay. I wonder if you hate me. I-I need your help. Maybe this is nothing. If it is, you can just keep the money. If it's serious I'm gonna need you. Like always."

"Okay." Sadie was shaking under Kat's touch. She grasped Kat's hand pulling it off her shoulder. "But I do this alone. I'll tell you if it's anything."

Kat nodded hesitantly, gently squeezing Sadie's hand still caught in her own. "Get some rest," she said. "You look exhausted." And with one more touch, she was gone, their fingers entwined till Kat was just out of reach. Then Sadie was alone in her office, nothing left of Kat but the faint scent of her perfume, her shampoo, her. Sadie sank into the nearest chair, collapsing into a heap. She felt on the brink of falling apart. Figuring it was the exhaustion, she dragged herself to a small room off the side of the office where she kept a small sofa and television for those late nights. In moments she was unconscious, drifting away from the chaos of the last 24 hours.

When she woke up her head was splitting. The clock resting above the television set read 2 pm. She groaned, rubbing her temple with the heel of her hand. Besides the table was a bottle of water, a container of aspirin standing next to it. Sadie picked the items up gratefully popping open the bottles, taking a long slug of water, and swallowing the pills along with it. Walking back to her desk she found Kat's check, slightly crumpled and spread on the desk next to a wrapped sandwich and a handwritten note. Sadie plucked the paper from the pile. It was Kat's handwriting. The letter said she figured Sadie might need some stuff when she woke. At the bottom was the address where she was staying. Signed 'love, Kat'. Sadie traced the words over again. Kat had called it surreal. It was accurate. Growing up Kat had been her entire world till she had broken her heart. Now here she was asking for help with something so direly important. And she was still so… beautiful. Sadie sighed, putting the letter down and grabbing the sandwich. She unwrapped it to find turkey and cheddar. What she liked growing up. She chuckled to herself. Kat was trying to be nice and it felt like a stab in the gut. She took a bite of the sandwich, grateful for one less thing to worry about.

Kat looked beautiful. Still delicate and graceful after all these years. It had been a common theme for her. She had met Kat when they were 6 years old. The very first day Kat moved into their neighborhood. They had lived in the same apartment building. Kat was short and pudgy. A feral little wild child. Sadie had been taller, all awkward angles and tangled hair. They had both been lonely kids. Finding each other had felt like a miracle. In any case, Sadie thanked whatever twist of fate that brought her friend into her life frequently in those days. They had grown up spending every day together till the friendship grew to something more and everything became far too complicated. Until everything broke.

Tracing Kat's handwriting with her fingertips she found the word *love*. Even then Kat had told her she loved her. It just hadn't been enough. Not enough to make her stay. Not enough to protect Kat from their shitty childhoods. Sadie picked the note up again. There was writing on the back. Flipping it over she saw where Kat had written the name of her dad's apartment alongside an address. Sadie stood rummaging around the cramped office for her boots and jacket. She found them in the adjacent room, placed neatly in a nearby chair. Kat must have removed them in her sleep. The familiarity of the gesture made her swallow hard.

Dressing and finding her wallet Sadie locked up the office, feeling ready to investigate Kat's father, one Todd Everett. The address Kat had left her wasn't very far. Exiting the building she felt thankful for the fresh air, and the relief it provided along with the aspirin. She walked and as she moved she wondered if there was a world where she would have ever said no to Kat. If there had ever been a time. Even when it hurt she always said yes. But things were different now. She stopped outside a grocery store, catching her reflection in the polished glass. She was different. She had changed so much from the little kid, from that teenage girl so desperately in love, eager to take love in whatever form Kat could give her. She couldn't do that now. But she could help her. For old time's sake. Because for their whole lives she had protected Kat. As best she could.

Arriving outside of Palmer Suites Sadie took in the dilapidated brick building that looked like the slightest touch would send it crumbling. It felt relatable. Sadie stood at the base of the apartment's steps, nestled between a laundromat and a pizza shop. Through the glass of the front door, she could make out the silhouette of someone coming down the stairs. Waiting till they were just close enough Sadie came jogging up the stairs grabbing the front door as it swung open. The person casually strolled out, scarcely noticing Sadie slip in behind them, avoiding the otherwise locked door. To the right of the front door were rows of mailboxes, affixed to each one a little white name tag displaying the surnames of the residents. None of the mailboxes said Everett. Sadie noticed a slot tucked beneath the boxes, inside a discarded flier for a used car lot, the name Todd Everett was typed neatly in the small white square. Apartment 7.

Climbing the stairs she scanned the apartments till finding the one in question. Lucky number 7. She approached the door reaching with closed fist to knock but stopped before making contact. The door was cracked open. Along its seam the lock had been broken, the wood splintered into shards around the silver metal brackets. She pushed the door open gently, listening closely for signs of life. Everything inside was deathly quiet. Opening the door wider Sadie stepped inside, half closing it behind her.

The place was sparse but nothing of value seemed taken. The sofa was askew, the coffee table overturned, but the television set was intact and on its perch. The telephone had been knocked to the floor where it remained, the handset lying adjacent from its cradle. Sadie picked both up, depositing them on a nearby table. The apartment was a studio scarcely the size of a shoebox and along the far wall was a mattress resting on the floor, the blanket and sheets a tangled heap atop the pallet. The wall beside it held a dresser, battered and bruised and clearly salvaged from a street corner. The drawers hung out haphazardly, clothes spilling out in waves, pouring onto the floor. The topmost drawer hung the furthest out, Sadie moved to close it, pressing in and feeling resistance. Her brow furrowed. Biting her lip she pulled instead, removing the drawer from its shelf and setting it on the floor. Reaching inside she felt paper affixed to the side, caught in the track. Pulling gently she freed it. A plane ticket for Todd Everett. One way to Brazil. Interesting travel choice. Kneeling down she glanced inside, catching a navy blue square taped to the back. Reaching in she grabbed it. A passport.

The soft creaky sounds of footsteps on old wood came from the doorway. Sadie tucked the documents into her jacket's interior pocket. Slowly she turned around, reaching for any obvious explanation for her presence. Standing in the doorway was Kat, caught in the milky sunlight pouring through the filthy windows. Her face was pinched, eyes wide as she surveyed the small disaster that was her father's apartment.

"I think he's okay," Sadie said. "It wasn't a robbery. Someone was looking for something. He wasn't here. From what I can tell."

Kat met her eyes, nodding along. Her brow relaxed though her wide eyes still seemed to be processing. "Where do you think he is?"

"I don't know," Sadie said. "But I found a plane ticket so he's looking to get out of town." She approached Kat, passing her the ticket and passport. She didn't reach for them. Sadie tucked them back in her pocket.

"I think it's as bad as I thought," Kat sighed, her shoulders slumped.

"What are you doing here?" Sadie asked, continuing to scan the apartment. "I thought I was doing this solo." On the other side of the bed was a small black box, laid open on the floor. Sadie walked over, cut into the box's interior was the shape of a handgun.

"I thought maybe I was overreacting," Kat said, watching Sadie.

"Apparently not," Sadie answered. Walking over to the phone she picked up the receiver and after a moment of searching her head dialed a number. Her phone began to vibrate in her pocket. She hung up the landline.

"What do we do now?" Kat asked. Sadie's mouth pinched into a grim line at the mention of 'we'.

"I'm going to that bar he called from," Sadie said pointedly. "You should go to your place. Wait for me to call you."

"The bar's not far from here. Maybe 3 or 4 blocks," Kat said, giving the apartment one last scan before turning and walking out the door. Sadie followed close behind shutting the broken door the best she could. Out in the hallway, Kat had been stopped by an elderly woman, her arms wrapped around a paper grocery bag. The woman was hurriedly chattering away as Kat nodded along politely. Sadie approached slipping easily alongside Kat.

"Hi. My name's Sadie Park, private investigator. I take it you live in this building."

The old woman eyeballed Sadie before replying, "Yes. Like I was telling this young lady, there was a break-in."

"I can tell that," Sadie said. "Did you see who broke into Mr. Everett's apartment?"

"Two large fellows," the woman said. "They came around before with Todd. This time Todd wasn't home, so they broke down the door. Only stayed a minute or two."

Sadie nodded along, before she could ask another question Kat interjected, "When was the last time you saw Todd?"

"A few days ago," the woman said, struggling to hold the bag. Sadie reached out, taking it from her. "Not unusual. He was always coming and going. Lately though...he seemed anxious. Worried."

"Thank you," Sadie said, reading the nervous look on Kat's face. She juggled the grocery bag to produce a business card, 'Daedalus Detective Agency' emblazoned in bold letters across the front. "If Mr. Everett shows up, have him give us a call."

"Who are you?" the old woman asked.

"I'm his daughter," Kat said simply. The old woman nodded, her eyes looking sorry as she took in Kat.

"Okay. I'll call," the woman said gently patting Kat's arm before stuffing the card in her purse. Taking the grocery bag back she tottered off to her apartment. Kat watched her unlock her door, juggling the bag on her hip. Sadie nudged her, tilting her head in the direction of the stairs. Kat turned following Sadie down the hallway and steps till they reached the front door. In her daze she couldn't help but stare, watching Sadie move, her black hair swaying as she walked, alive and right in front of her. No longer confined to the millions of memories Kat had clung to all these years. Sadie reached to open the door, instinctively Kat reached too, her hand resting atop Sadie's, stopping her movement.

"I'm scared," Kat said, locking eyes with her.

Sadie's heart ached with how small Kat looked in that instant. "Don't be. I'm right here with you." Together they opened the door. Sadie kept her hand for an instant, pulling Kat along in the direction they needed to go in. Kat followed close along the sidewalk, every now and again her fingers grazing Sadie's, neither acknowledging the touches when they occurred. She had sudden flashes of being a 15-year-old girl, walking down similar streets, feeling hopelessly lost in her best friend.

"Tell me honestly," Kat said, breaking the silence between them. "What do you think is going on?"

"Honestly?" Sadie slowed her pace, taking in Kat's profile, her distracted gaze as she followed Sadie along. "I think he owes someone a lot of money. And I think he's trying to skip town before anything bad happens."

"Do you think he's safe?" Kat asked, looking directly at Sadie now.

"Yes," Sadie answered. "Whoever they are, they want their money. Do you want to call the cops? File a missing person report?"

"No." Kat shook her head. "I don't want to be the reason my dad goes to jail. I don't even know what he looks like anymore."

"Here." Sadie dug in her jacket producing the passport. She handed it to Kat who took it this time.

"Thank you," Kat said, clutching it without opening it, pausing a moment before sliding it in the purse slung over her shoulder. They came to a stop outside a rundown bar, its windows blotted out with posters and signage.

"This is the place," Sadie said. Kat nodded eyes transfixed on the other woman, "I still think you should go home."

"Are you going to make me?" Kat asked, casting her eyes up to the bar's gently glowing neon sign.

"I could never make you do anything." Sadie laughed, easing the mood. "But since you're determined." She pulled the door open holding it for Kat and with a wave of her hand indicated for her to go in first.

Kat chuckled, shaking her head and reaching to touch Sadie's arm as she passed her, entering the dim cavern of the bar. Sadie followed suit letting the door swing shut behind her, extinguishing the daylight. The darkness gave way to dim lights and neon signs glowing against the barroom walls.

Mostly it was empty except for a handful of solitary drunks nursing their cups in separate corners. Behind the bar was a woman, tall and lean, her skin a rich brown with a half sleeve of tattoos poking out from her loose t-shirt. Kat began approaching the bar when she noticed Sadie was no longer beside her. Turning she saw the other woman standing still, looking past her at the bartender. Her mouth was pressed in that grim line that used to make Kat worry when they were kids.

"Are you okay?" Kat asked, wanting to reach out and comfort her. Restraining herself, she waited, silently reading Sadie.

"Yeah," she said. "I... let me handle this, okay?" Kat nodded reluctantly before finding a stool on the far end of the bar. Sadie watched her, struck by her graceful movements. She approached the bartender alone. "Hey, Andy," Sadie said, drawing the woman's attention. Her warm amber eyes took Sadie in and she gave a familiar half-smile.

"Hey," she answered. "Wasn't expecting to see you today." Andy leaned against the bar top.

"I'm working a new case," Sadie replied, unable to help smiling back at Andy.

"Oh." Andy turned to look at Kat before returning her attention to Sadie. "Okay."

"I'm looking for a guy named Todd Everett."

"Seems to be a hot topic lately," Andy said. "A girl called asking about him the other day."

"I know." Sadie leaned against the bar. "She's his daughter." Sadie searched Andy's face, all the familiar features she had grown so fond of. A subtle realization bloomed across Andy.

"Kat? Everett. Not that Kat Everett?" Andy asked, eyes wide as she stared at Sadie. Sadie nodded. Andy looked back at the end of the bar, thoroughly assessing Kat who remained unaware, turning a dark blue passport over and over again. "Can we talk in private?"

Sadie followed Andy around the bar into a small corridor. Andy gestured to a barback who gave a thumbs up before going in front. Andy led them to a back office, ushering Sadie in before shutting the door behind them.

"You brought your ex to your other ex's bar?"

"She's technically not my ex," Sadie said, tucking her hands in her jacket pockets. "And I didn't ask her to come along."

"Todd's her dad?" Andy asked. "Must be rough."

"She hasn't seen him since she was 10. He called her, got her all shook up," Sadie answered, looking at the shut door as if she could see Kat beyond it.

"Are you okay with all this?" Andy said, drawing her attention.

"I can't just leave her on her own."

At the bar Kat sat clutching onto the passport, still turning it over and over. She was so intent on the little booklet that she hadn't noticed the other bartender was standing in front of her asking if she wanted anything and was startled from her racing thoughts. She looked up seemingly lost as she stared at the man. Fumbling for a response she stared at the rows of bottles lining the barroom wall. The pit of her stomach went cold and she swallowed feeling the sudden pangs of yearning.

"No," she answered, shaking her head. "Um. A club soda." She smiled briefly, half-heartedly at the bartender. He smiled back winking at her before turning away to grab a glass. Kat ignored his departure, instead fixating on the passport. She ran her fingertips delicately along the engraved letters. Opening it revealed the usual pages. She flipped casually till she came to the photo page where suddenly her father's face was staring back at her. The same eyes, the same crooked smile, charming the camera even in a boring government document. His face was so much older than she remembered. His eyes were still youthful but his face was etched with lines, the skin starting to sag, his hair starting to thin at the top. It must have embarrassed him so much. The information below listed a midwestern home. It must match the phone number he gave her. The issue date was four years ago. He must have been 50 in the photo. He had been in his 30s the last time she'd seen him. An energetic man ready to take on the world, constantly on the move. He was full of mischief and laughter. Kat wondered if that was still the case. He had certainly gotten into some things in the years. Her fingers ran along the house address, her mind flooding with memories of that peculiar phone call. The fraught woman on the other end of the line asked if she'd seen Todd, if she could pass a message along. The curious boy who'd answered before surrendering the phone. The bartender returned, producing the glass in front of her. Asking if she needed anything else. She shook her head no, dismissing the man.

"What does she know?" Andy asked.

"I'm not sure," Sadie said, looking around the office, afraid to meet Andy's gaze, scared all the phantom pain that had sprung up today would send her unraveling. "She only turned up this morning."

"Does she know about us?" she asked, gesturing between the two. "Does she know what happened?" The second question was quieter, scarcely above a whisper.

Sadie's eyes narrowed. "That hardly matters. I'm just helping her find Todd, then she'll be back out of town with her girlfriend and we won't talk anymore."

"Is she still with that woman? The cougar." Andy asked. Sadie's sudden bark of laughter filled the office. Andy couldn't tell if it was genuine or sarcastic.

"I guess so," Sadie said, feeling a sudden stab in the gut at the thought. "Can you just help me out so I can get this over with?"

"You should talk to her," Andy said, resting a hand on Sadie's shoulder. "Might be your only shot at closure." Sadie shook her head, a tear came trickling down her face before falling from her chin. "And you know it doesn't have to be the end. You can ask her to stay in touch."

Sadie bit her lip, blinking away more tears. "I don't know."

"You never thought about it?" Andy asked. "Don't answer. I know you have." Then she laughed like it was a joke. She took her hand from Sadie's arm. "Todd started coming in 6 or 7 months ago. Off and on. He said he worked on the road. In shipping. Some big, tough looking guys came in a few times to talk with him. Someone said they were the mob"

"Did you get their names?" Sadie asked.

"No," Andy said, voice falling even. "How have you been? Aside from work."

"Fine," Sadie sighed. "It's been quiet."

"So you're overthinking," Andy said, her face breaking out into a playful, chiding smile, before turning more serious once again. "I've missed you. Feels like even when you're here, you're not here. You know what I mean?" Sadie nodded solemnly, unable to answer. Andy went to the door, opened it, and stepped back into the hallway. Sadie followed her out. "Call me when you're done with this," Andy continued. "I want to talk to her alone before you go." Andy smirked, rushing ahead.

Sadie lingered running through the litany of things Andy could say to Kat. Her eyes widened, filling with fear. She chased after entering the bar room only to see Andy already approaching Kat from behind the bar, sparking up a conversation while Kat ran a finger along the edge of her glass, its ice cubes clinking together as it moved. She looked past Andy meeting Sadie's eyes. Sadie swallowed, unsure what was passing through Kat's head.

"So you're Kat?" Andy said, leaning against the bar top.

"Yes. I think we spoke on the phone. Andrea, right?" Kat asked, still playing with the glass.

"That's me," Andy said. "You need a refill?"

"I'm ok," Kat answered, smiling pleasantly at Andy, taking in her pretty features and elegant movements. "Do you know Sadie?"

"I do," Andy said, smiling at Kat. "We used to go out." Kat's smile fell subtly, her eyes shrinking, suddenly scrutinizing Andy while attempting to hide it. "You should be careful. While you're here. She's more fragile than you think. And you don't know what's happened since you've been gone. You really did a number on her," Andy sighed, acutely aware of Sadie's eyes on her back.

"How long were you together?" Kat asked, voice composed and deliberate.

"Two years. Give or take."

"I know I hurt her," Kat began, shoulders slumping. "I was a selfish kid. I'm probably still that selfish. But I'm not here to hurt her. I couldn't stand the thought."

Andy looked down, kicking with the toe of her shoe at the corner of a rubber mat, its surface slick with water. "I hope you find your dad. He seems like a nice guy." Andrea walked away to tend to another patron.

From the far end of the bar Sadie nodded for Kat to come along. She nodded back feeling a familiar warmth spread across her. A subtle pull that drew her to Sadie. She left her seat leaving a few dollars on the wooden counter and crossed the room.

"Hey," she said, her voice faint against the dull noise of the bar's tv playing aimlessly in the background.

"You ready to go?" Sadie asked.

Kat nodded back letting Sadie open the door for her. "What'd she say?" She stepped outside, watching Sadie follow close behind, the fading sunlight catching her, making her glow in the evening light.

"Todd's been coming around the last 6 months. He told her he worked in shipping. She saw him hanging around with some bad looking guys." Sadie watched Kat closely, trying to read the colliding emotions on her face. "I'm gonna see if I can chase down a lead on these guys. I need to go alone though.

Do you want me to walk you home?"

Kat turned, catching the fading sun against the city skyline. "I'll call a car," Kat said. She stepped closer to Sadie touching her arm gently. "We'll talk later." She gave her a half-smile before stepping closer, kissing her so softly on the cheek that Sadie could scarcely feel the warm press of skin against her. Then Kat was gone, retreating down the sidewalk.

"This is so fucking crazy," Sadie sighed, turning in the opposite direction.

The walk to her apartment wasn't too long. She figured she'd take the scenic route, if you could call it that. She felt overwhelmed by everything the last 24 hours had brought. She wondered what Andy had said to Kat. Wondered what Kat could possibly be thinking. Wondered where the fuck Todd was. Apparently he'd gotten himself involved with the mob and, for some foolish reason, chose to involve his daughter. He didn't deserve her. Never had. Though it hadn't been a blessing the day he disappeared from Kat's life. Somehow things in Kat's home grew worse. Sadie could never squeeze the details from Kat of what transpired to turn her so quiet, to mute the life in her eyes when they were younger. More times Sadie didn't protect her. She watched the faces of people passing as she navigated the familiar streets. She'd only spent a few short hours with Kat and she was missing her already. She could still feel the ghost sensation of her lips against her cheek. Sadie wished she was mad at Kat, her long lost friend. She just felt sad. And vaguely queasy. The evening air was already beginning to take on a chill. Sadie wrapped her jacket tighter around herself feeling grateful to see her apartment at the end of the street.

Her phone started to ring aggressively in her pocket. She absently pulled the device out glancing at the plastic screen. Detective Daniel Guinto. Just who she needed. Though she began to fear she'd never make it home.

"Just the man I wanted," Sadie said, answering her phone, bringing it to her ear and tucking herself to the edge of the sidewalk.

"Coming on to me is highly unprofessional," Daniel said, voice laced with mirth. "What do you need, Park?"

"I'm working a missing person case. I think the mob is involved."

"Let's grab a cup of coffee," Daniel replied, the mirth quickly fading. "The regular place."

"Sure," Sadie said before hanging up. She stared longingly at her apartment before turning down an adjacent street. When she had occasion to meet with Daniel it was at a coffee shop three blocks away. Danny was a cop on the force like his dad. Daniel's dad used to work with Hector, before Hector left the force. Hector was like an uncle to Danny so when Sadie asked for help on a case he didn't mind.

When she arrived the sun had completely disappeared giving way to an inky night sky, the light pollution blotting out the possibility of stars. The moon hung high above, peering down at Sadie. Daniel was already inside sitting alone in a booth sipping a cup of coffee. Sadie entered the shop, the bell affixed above the door chiming, announcing her arrival. Daniel looked up, catching sight of her immediately. His black hair was mussed and his dark eyes were tired as he took in Sadie's appearance. As she sat Danny signaled the waitress who got to work pouring a cup of coffee.

"How are you?" Daniel asked.

"Tired," Sadie said, smiling at the waitress as she deposited the coffee in front of her. "Thank you."

"What's your case?" Daniel sipped his own coffee, squinting at Sadie.

Sadie toyed with the cup, turning it slowly, feeling the heat burn through the ceramic and warm her fingertips. "Looking for a friend's dad. He was last seen with some bad people. Might be mob. Was hoping you could I.D. them for me."

"Okay," Daniel said, setting the mug down, and leaning an elbow on the tabletop. "You think your friend's dad got tangled up with the mob?"

"Sounds like him." Sadie sipped her coffee, grateful for the warmth. "Some guys were seen at his apartment and broke in. Two big guys. I don't have names. They're probably involved in some kind of trafficking."

Daniel nodded. The waitress appeared producing a slice of cherry pie with a dollop of whipped cream piled on top. He thanked the woman, who smiled warmly at him, before taking a bite. "Who's your friend's dad?" He asked, mouth half full with dessert.

Sadie hesitated. Kat hadn't wanted to involve cops. But they were short on leads and Kat wanted to find Todd, presumably before he got hurt. Or worse. "Stays between us?" Daniel rolled his eyes before nodding his agreement. Sadie didn't say anything.

"Do you want me to pinky swear?" he asked playfully.

"It's important."

"Fine. I promise," Daniel said, pushing the plate away.

"His name's Todd Everett."

After a moment's pause, Daniel answered, "The name sounds familiar. I'll look into it, get back to you later." Sadie nodded. Daniel stood producing a few bills and placing them on the table between the emptied dishes. He waved to the waitress before turning to go.

"Thank you," Sadie said before he left. Daniel just grinned at her before leaving the cafe, the shop door jingling in his wake. Sadie lingered a moment finishing her coffee. The waitress came by again brandishing a coffee pot, and offering a refill. In her free hand she held a Styrofoam container.

"Slice of pie. On the house," the woman said, sliding the box on the table. "You look like you've had a rough one."

"I think today's haunted." Sadie laughed, thanking her for the pie before disappearing out the front door. The night had grown cold fast and the walk home was thankfully brief.

Sadie stumbled into her apartment glad to finally see it again. She kicked her boots off at the door, tossing them aside before making her way into the kitchen, opening the motley fridge, and depositing the pie in exchange for some leftover Chinese food. Finding a fork in the sink she rinsed it off before opening the lid and taking a hearty bite. Setting the container down she peeled her jacket off, tossing it onto a nearby chair. The apartment was a sea of silence. It felt like the first quiet she'd had all day. The solace washed over her. She produced a can of soda from the fridge, popping the top and taking a prolonged swig, feeling droplets of soda on the corners of her mouth. Grabbing the can and the container she headed into her bedroom, depositing her makeshift dinner onto the nightstand. She ran a hand through her hair. A shower seemed in order.

Sadie entered the bathroom across from her bedroom flicking the light switch and flooding the room in the fluorescent glow, the gentle hum of the light filling her ears. With a few twists of the knobs, the shower came to life adding the sound of water droplets to the night. Sadie pulled her shirt over her head, feeling stiffness in her shoulders, the wear of stress becoming evident. Kat showing up unexpectedly had thrown her so terribly off-kilter. In this brief, private moment, she could finally breathe, finally get her footing in a world spinning out of control. She wondered how Kat was feeling. It's funny how even after all this time she still worried about Kat's feelings first. The heat of the water enveloped Sadie. Her soap began to perfume the air, soothing her nerves. Today was over. And she could finally sleep in her own bed, locked away from the world in her own bubble. She sighed letting the water wash away a day that had been too laden with history. She shut the shower off feeling heavy with sleep and wrapped a towel around herself.

She collapsed into the bed stretching out on her back and staring at the ceiling. Forgetting about her dinner she reached into the nightstand drawer producing a small stack of photos, the edges worn down and frayed with age. Sadie plucked the photo from the back and placed the rest down next to her bedside lamp. Turning on her side she stared at the photograph. Depicted in the aging ink was Sadie with an arm casually draped around Kat. They were 16 in the photograph, faces rounder, eyes brighter. Kat shined bright in the photo, filled with a life that bloomed out of the paper like a magic charm. Back then Sadie was painfully processing so much she didn't understand about herself. The multitude of ways she felt, the sudden things she found herself wanting. Her best friend Kat, being one of them. She remembered her heart aching every day to be close to her, feeling so terrified back then. She didn't even know all the secrets Kat had been keeping. All of them broke her heart in some way. She remembered Kat telling her she loved her in frenzied whispers, Kat loving her, Kat leaving. Eventually for good, with some woman Sadie didn't know. But she loved Kat too, and she had money and a way for Kat to escape the crushing sadness of the lives they were born into. It didn't stop her from thinking about Kat. Apparently, Kat had thought of her too. Sadie sat the photo down with the rest. Sleep overwhelmed her till her eyes drifted shut and she was lost to the day, surrendering to the exhaustion.

Chapter Two

It was a sweltering summer day, all around Sadie and Kat kids were screaming and laughing. Their raucous joy infiltrated the street, singing to every pedestrian that passed. A half-block away children had busted open a fire hydrant, its contents spilling everywhere in torrential spray cooling the pavement, sending vapor into the air in cloudy swirls that hung above the road before spiraling off into the sky. Children ran in and out of the water spray, laughing hysterically. The world was alive all around them. Kat was walking slightly ahead, her auburn hair turning red in the sun's sharp rays. Sadie's eyes were drawn to her. Like always. They could be in the middle of a crowded room and her eyes would always search out her beautiful best friend. Kat turned back to look at her, clear blue eyes dancing in the light. She smiled, all her teeth showing in a dazzling display. Sadie's heart fluttered. They were approaching a crowded section of sidewalk. Kat reached back, grasping Sadie's hand, entwining their fingers. Something they had done a million times before. It was different this time. The simplest touch sent Sadie's heart racing. She squeezed Kat's hand, feeling the connection shoot through her.

The pair pressed through the crowd, Sadie keeping close to

her back. She suddenly felt scared of losing Kat in the crush of bodies surrounding them. For moments she couldn't see the other girl, though she could feel her hand wrapped in her own, tethering them together. They reached the other side and there Kat was. Waiting. Sadie felt her foot catch on something, an errant crack of cement on the sidewalk. She stumbled and Kat's outstretched arms were there to catch her. She felt Kat's arm wrap around her waist. Keeping her steady. Keeping her upright. Their faces were painfully close. Sadie felt overcome with the urge to kiss Kat. She had thought about it for a long time now. She'd never been kissed before and in her quiet moments alone when she thought about what that experience might be like all she could see was Kat. Her lips, her round eyes, her sweet soft voice. All the girls they knew at school talked incessantly about the boys they kissed or wanted to kiss. She shook her head free of the thought.

Kat released her waist. A faint blush colored her cheeks. She still held onto Sadie's hand, their fingers weaved together. They navigated the rest of the walk, hands entwined. They spoke casually about summer break and the things they might do. They were going to the library. Sadie had walked Kat there every week since they were little. They picked out books together, sometimes picking ones out for each other, like little gifts. This time she picked a book of poems for Kat. She had never been much for poetry but something about the slim little volume called to her. She had watched Kat read it in Sadie's dingy little bedroom, curled up in her bed, her ancient stereo straining music through its tiny speakers. Kat cried and it broke Sadie's heart. She started to apologize, suddenly overcome with fear that she'd done the wrong thing. Kat thanked her, wiping the tears away she said it was beautiful. She kissed Sadie on the cheek. She had never felt so loved. Even though Kat never said it.

Sadie startled awake, ears ringing, heart racing in her chest, thumping against her ribcage in protest. She was breathing hard trying to make sense of the still dark room. Slowly she registered the phone ringing obnoxiously on her nightstand. She blindly grasped for it, the screen's bright light blurring her vision. Sadie answered, putting the call on speaker and rubbing her burning eyes.

"Sadie?" Kat's voice filtered through the line, her voice strained. Sadie could recognize the masked tears, the crack in her voice making Sadie swallow hard. "I need you to call off the investigation."

Sadie squinted in the dark making out her alarm clock reading 5:28 am. "What's going on?" The line fell painfully silent. After a long, pregnant moment, Kat spoke.

"Some guys came here. They were looking for Dad. Asked if I'd seen him," Kat said, voice trembling through her efforts to be calm.

"Did they threaten you?" Sadie asked.

"N-n-not exactly," Kat stammered. "I'm fine. But I think maybe we should-"

"I'm coming over." Sadie stood from her bed scrambling for

the nearest clothes. "Do you want me to stay on the phone?" She struggled to pull her jeans on, nearly tripping in her hurry.

"N-no," Kat sighed. "How long will you be?"

"30 minutes," Sadie said, finding a shirt bunched up on top of her dresser. "Keep the doors locked."

"Okay," Kat said, voice filling the room. "Be safe." Then she was gone, the line falling dead.

Sadie grabbed the phone tucking it in her back pocket. Scrambling out of her bedroom on autopilot she found her jacket and shoes. Her mind was racing faster than her feet could carry her. She swallowed her fear bracing herself for the city streets. Sadie ran, feet hitting the pavement, the loudest sound in the empty morning dark. She ran until she could find a cab, hopping into the back she barked the address at the driver. He grumbled indistinctly before pulling off maneuvering swiftly through streets barely coming to life.

The sun was beginning to crest the horizon when Sadie came stumbling out of the taxi, carelessly tossing bills at him before he went speeding off. She rushed into the building, finding the elevator on the opposite end of the lobby. She pressed the call button over and over hoping to hurry its arrival. After achingly painful moments she abandoned the elevator, finding the stairwell instead. She climbed till her legs were aching and her lungs were ready to burst from her ribcage, till suddenly she found herself at Kat's door. She paused, taking a breath to steady herself. She knocked. The door opened quickly and there Kat was, eyes red-rimmed and raw, the tip of her nose red. She sniffled through a smile at the sight of Sadie. A weak half-smile, more relief than joy. Sadie surged forward taking Kat in her arms, feeling the weight of her.

"Are you okay?" She whispered, face pressed into Kat's hair.

Kat nodded against her, clinging onto her taller frame. Sadie felt warm droplets of tears fall onto her cheek. She pulled back, one arm still wrapped around Kat and searched her face, taking a hand and brushing messy locks of hair behind her ear. She pulled the other woman back in, kissing her forehead. Kat cradled her head into Sadie's neck. After long moments Kat's breathing slowed. Sadie felt herself stop trembling. The scent of Kat surrounded her, the warmth and weight of her body against her own. The wave of relief at the sensation of her. Kat. Right here. Right now. Like a dream clouding her vision. Any moment she'd wake up to the lingering scent of her. She had missed her so much. 10 years of missing her. Sadie couldn't fight that breathless feeling, the same one she felt when they had been teens.

Kat didn't look any less spooked. She pulled away. Her eyes searched Sadie, taking every inch of her in, recommitting her to memory. Kat was still as she watched Sadie shut the door behind her and stand in the foyer, long black hair framing her face, all sharp angles and full lips. She felt a flood of relief and wanted to laugh. Funny how not even time had erased the sensation, that feeling of safety around the other woman. She wanted to pull her close again, to feel her body again, know she was really here. Instead, she stayed still. Waiting for Sadie.

Still feeling scared that she'd vanish right before her.

"You're here," was all Kat could manage.

"I was worried about you," Sadie said, getting closer, so close Kat could smell her soap, her shampoo, the underlying familiar scent of her.

"Some things never change." Kat locked eyes with Sadie, smiling that same playful smile that always disarmed her.

Holding back the tide of questions rushing through her, Sadie reached out taking Kat in her arms, closing the gap between them. Kat melted into the embrace, wrapping her arms around Sadie, she pulled her impossibly close, and when she pulled away Sadie's eyes were rimmed with tears. With a shaky hand, she caressed her cheek, silently wiping tears away.

"It's okay. I'm here," Sadie whispered, voice faint against the quiet. They stood stuck in the embrace for endless moments before Kat found herself and taking Sadie by the hand led her to the living room. She took a seat on the lush sofa and with a simple gesture invited Sadie to sit. She slid in next to Kat, tucking her hands into her jacket pockets, keeping herself from reaching for Kat. It didn't matter. Kat was pressed against her, slipping back into the easy regard they had so long ago. "What's going on?" Sadie asked.

"I woke up in the middle of the night. 2 AM maybe. There was a knock at the door. I wasn't thinking," Kat said, looking away as she remembered. "I opened the door and they forced their way in."

"And you're okay?" Sadie asked, taking Kat by the chin to look at her.

"Y-yes." Kat whispered. "They were asking about Dad. Demanded to see him. I had to convince them I didn't know."

"You got a good look at them?" Sadie asked. Kat nodded. "You could give a description."

"Jaime has cameras. In the foyer. And the hallways."

Sadie's face grew stony at the mention of Jaime. "Makes sense."

"I can show you," Kat said, noting the subtle shift in tone. She stood, trusting Sadie to follow her out of the room and further into the apartment. They entered a small office, a large window on the far wall overlooked the street below. Through the glass the sun was lighting the sky in streaks of red and pink that bloomed outwards, the clouds dotting the sky catching it and adopting its color before fading back to white. Kat took a seat at the desk and began pressing buttons, knowing exactly what to do. Sadie watched the marks of focus on her face, the way her brow furrowed, the look of clarity in her piercing eyes. The sunrise made her glow, the computer's screen illuminated her face in white light. Sadie tried to steady herself against the thoughts colliding in her head, threatening to overwhelm her. She shut her eyes to the world breathing in, then out in steady fashion. Something Andy had taught her years ago, in darker times. In. Then out. She narrowed the world down to her own breaths, the small clicks of the computer, the subtle sounds of Kat's breathing, letting it ground her. Slowly she opened her eyes. Kat had stopped her tinkering on the computer. She sat silently watching Sadie.

"Come here." She tilted her head asking for her to come closer. Sadie rounded the desk standing beside Kat, peering down at the screen. Kat scrubbed through the video finding the beginning, when the men knocked on the door. "I don't think there's sound."

"That's okay," Sadie said.

Kat pressed play.

She appeared walking across the screen, wrapped in a robe, hair messy and tangled in the back. Without hesitation Kat opened the door, the chain still locked, strung across the gap. The door came swinging open forcefully breaking the metal. Kat came stumbling back, tripping, and falling to the floor. Two men entered, tall with square shoulders and broad faces, one with a hook nose and dark hair, the other was bald with a scar cut across his chin. Both wore dark clothes with jackets over top. Hook nose grabbed Kat from the floor holding her aloft like she was a rag doll and pinning her to the wall. The bald guy spoke. Kat said something back. The whole affair was only minutes. The bald man disappeared returning after a few tense moments where the man still pining Kat to the wall eyeballed her salaciously. They left.

Kat paused the video, looking away from the screen. Sadie

rested a hand on Kat's shoulder, her jaw clenched tight. Gently she pulled Kat into an embrace, Kat wrapping her arms around Sadie's hips. Sadie knelt down, eyes wet and sparkling in the early morning sun.

"You're really brave, Kat," she whispered, face so close to Kat's she could feel her breath against her. "Can you get this on a flash drive?" Kat nodded, opening a desk drawer and digging around till she produced the small device. Sadie stayed kneeling while Kat turned away. After a few moments of decisive clicking, she closed the windows and turned the computer off. Sadie watched her closely. "Did you sleep?"

"Not after." Kat sighed, slipping her the drive.

"Do you still want to stop looking for Todd?" Sadie asked, taking Kat's hand in her own.

"He's in trouble," she said. "I want to help him."

Sadie nodded. "I need to go show this to someone. It'll help us find him."

"I don't want to stay here," Kat said. "Not alone."

"You can stay with me," Sadie whispered. "At my place." Kat stroked her cheek at the words. Sadie bit her own lip, stressing it with her teeth. "You should grab your stuff."

Kat nodded, standing. Sadie stood grasping Kat's hand, helping her up, the chair scraping against the floor as it moved back.

Kat stared deeply into Sadie's eyes, hand still in Sadie's. For a moment they stood there in the silence, sunlight flooding into the room from behind them. Slowly Sadie released her. Kat turned, leaving the room to pack. Sadie took a deep breath exhaling through her nose, watching the empty space where Kat had been.

How did this go from bad to worse?

She ran a hand through her hair. Pulling her phone from her pocket she dialed Daniel's number. The line rang and rang endlessly before a grumbled tired voice came filtering into her ear.

"Mhhph-hello," Daniel said, groggy from sleep.

"Danny! I got video of the guys I'm looking for. Can I bring it to you?"

"Sure," Daniel answered, sounding only half aware. "I have to be at the station. Can you meet me there?"

"Yeah," Sadie said, still staring at the empty doorway. "I'll be there soon." She heard Daniel mumble something before hanging up.

Stepping into the hallway Sadie followed the sounds of movement till she found the bedroom. She leaned against the door frame watching Kat shift things into an overnight bag. She disappeared into the nearby bathroom unaware that Sadie could see the reflection of her face in the mirror. She looked so drained. It made Sadie's heart ache. Nothing she'd ever imagined had prepared her for this. Kat knelt over the bathroom sink twisting the faucet on, splashing handfuls of water on her face. She blindly reached for a nearby towel to dry her face. Tossing the towel aside she collected a toothbrush and toothpaste before returning to the bedroom.

"I have to make a stop. On the way to my place."

"Okay," Kat said, giving her a tired smile before tossing her toiletries into the bag. She grabbed a jacket from the bed shrugging it on before collecting her belongings. She slung it on one shoulder before approaching Sadie. "I'm ready." Sadie put a hand out gesturing for the bag. Kat rolled her eyes, smiling before handing it over to Sadie.

On the street corner, Sadie patiently waited, arm outstretched in an attempt to hail a cab for them. Kat stood close by, arms wrapped tightly around herself. Soon a yellow taxi was pulled alongside them and Sadie was taking her by the hand, guiding her into the car. Kat slid into the seat with Sadie close behind, shutting the door firmly behind her, and setting the bag down next to the door. Sadie told the driver where to go and they pulled off crossing overcrowded streets through the city. Kat stared out the window watching row after row of buildings pass, the streets overflowing with people. It felt like a distant memory come to life. She could feel Sadie's eyes on her. She felt choked with all the things she wanted to tell Sadie. Of course she was dumb enough to waltz back into Sadie's life unannounced and pull her into all of this..mess. Her eyes started to burn and her breath hitched. She felt a warm hand reach out, touching her own in comfort. She turned from the window to see Sadie.

"I'm sorry," Kat whispered, meeting Sadie's gaze. "I always make such a mess." A tear spilled from her landing on the stained seat.

"It's not your fault," Sadie said, sliding closer to Kat in the backseat till they were pressed together. "We got this, right? You and me."

Kat chuckled quietly. "Alright." She stared back out the window to see the police station outside. The car came to a slow stop in an empty space. "Where are we?"

"I'm going to give the video to my friend. He can tell us who these guys are. If we're lucky," Sadie said. "I can't tell you what to do, but you can file a report."

"N-no," Kat said, shaking her head.

"Then wait here." Sadie squeezed her hand. "I won't be long."

Kat nodded, feeling Sadie's fingers fall away. She watched her go, sinking further into the seat, her eyes following as Sadie approached an Asian man in a trim-cut gray suit on the other side of the building. Her thoughts drifted back to the apartment. Sadie had seemed stung by the mention of Jaime. Reasonably so. She sighed to herself. Sadie had always disliked Jaime and their 'unusual' relationship. At this point the older woman had been so enmeshed in her life for so long that it was hard to gloss over her presence, interwoven so finely into Kat's life. After all, Jaime was a part of who she'd become over the years. But maybe this baggage was a place to start to unravel all the things she still owed Sadie.

On the stairs of the police station, Sadie slipped Daniel the flash drive. He glanced over her shoulder at the waiting taxi. "Can you call me? As soon as you know something."

Daniel nodded. "Is that your client? Is she okay?"

"Yeah," Sadie sighed, looking around at the multitude of cops coming and going. "I think she'll be better when this is over."

"I bet," Daniel said. "Keep her safe. I'll call later." He tucked the drive into his pocket, turning and climbed the stairs, disappearing into the frenzied building.

Sadie ran back to the car slipping into the backseat alongside Kat.

"Hey, thanks," she said to the driver. "Can you get us to 5850 Willard?" The driver made a gruff noise and pulled away from the curb. Sadie leaned back into her seat, sighing and rubbing her eyes, feeling a wave of tiredness creep up on her.

"Sadie," Kat said, voice so quiet it took Sadie a moment to realize she'd spoken. "This is all such shitty timing."

"I'll say." Sadie laughed sardonically.

"About Jaime," Kat continued, feeling Sadie tense beside her. "We broke up. A-a year ago." Kat felt her nerves begin to get the better of her, the sudden sensation of Sadie's gaze making it all the worse. "We're still friends. She's still important to me. But… it's not like that. Not anymore."

There was a long pause. The car suddenly filled with silence.

"Are you okay?" Sadie asked. Kat smiled at her. A soft, gentle, warm smile. Out the window, the gentle patter of rain began to drop onto the car.

"It was a while ago." She glanced out the window, seeing the water pebble on the glass before falling in streaks. "It doesn't rain where I live. You forget how beautiful it can be."

"I always liked the rain. Makes everything peaceful. Like the world can finally rest." Sadie smiled at Kat, eyes crinkling at the edges. "Like when we were kids and we'd watch movies in our PJs."

Kat laughed. "Better times."

Sadie nodded. They weren't, but they could pretend. The taxi slowed outside Sadie's apartment building. Kat dug some bills from her purse and handed them to the driver, thanking him as they exited the vehicle. Sadie opened the front door holding it open for Kat. She walked in letting Sadie guide her up the stairs to the small apartment.

"This is me," Sadie said, unlocking the door. "It's not much, but it's home." Sadie stepped inside letting Kat in.

"It's wonderful." Kat looked around the room, taking in all the little details of Sadie's home. The art on the walls, the books on shelves, the places where the mess of everyday life accumulated.

Sadie laughed. "You're crazy."

"It's yours," Kat said, voice sincere. "So it's wonderful."

Sadie looked away feeling a blush creep across her cheeks. "You're probably exhausted." She deposited Kat's bag on the sofa. "You can sleep in my bed. I'll show you." Kat followed her through the living room to the bedroom. Being surrounded by so much of the other woman soothed her, made everything seem more manageable. Sadie didn't bother turning on a light. She pointed out the bathroom. "If you want to change."

"Thanks,"Kat said before disappearing to get her things.

Sadie sat on the bed, kicking off her boots and slipping her jacket off. Having Kat here suddenly felt too intimate. And now she knew Jaime was out of the picture. Did that even matter? It didn't change the past. Even if she had spent years rationalizing it to herself. It didn't change anything that happened. All the hurt when she had been here, all the hurt in her long absence. Kat returned wearing a pair of shorts and a t-shirt. Sadie stood pulling the blankets down for her.

"You don't have to do that," Kat said.

"You're right." Sadie stopped herself, abandoning the task. "I guess I wanted to."

Kat sat on the edge of the bed close to Sadie. "Thank you," she said, searching her face.

"It's okay," Sadie said, turning to go, "I'll give you some space."

"Could you-" Kat said. "Could you stay with me awhile?" Sadie nodded, watching Kat stretch out under the blanket. She lay alongside her, feeling the warmth of her body. Kat turned so she was face to face with Sadie, "I'm so tired," Kat sighed, eyes heavy as she settled into the pillows, "Can I- " Kat started then cut herself off, letting the unfinished words hang between them.

"What?" Sadie asked patiently.

"Can I get closer?" Kat asked, voice suddenly meek. Sadie's eyebrows knit together in mild confusion. She nodded hesitantly curious about her intent. Kat slid closer till her entire body was pressed into Sadie's side, she tucked her head under Sadie's chin, her face coming to rest along her collarbone. Sadie wrapped an arm around her, cradling her. She swallowed hard. "I can-I can move," Kat said.

"No," Sadie replied. "You're fine. Just get some rest." Kat nodded nuzzling into the space she'd created for herself. Slowly she drifted to sleep in Sadie's arms. Sadie couldn't help but kiss her forehead, letting her lips linger there for a moment. In her half-asleep state Kat casually draped an arm

51

along Sadie's waist. She felt helpless and quickly faded into a dream, soothed by the weight of the other woman on her, the relief of knowing she was safe. She hated herself for feeling so disarmed. She squeezed Kat gently, reaffirming that she was real. Really here. Not a fever dream.

"I missed you," Kat mumbled.

"I missed you too," Sadie answered.

Soon Kat was asleep. Sadie could only lay there half underneath the other woman. She was left alone with her thoughts, a surge of information bouncing around her tired mind. Kat wasn't with Jaime. Hadn't been for some time. Kat was on top of her. In her arms. She needed to rethink every interaction she'd had with her long-lost friend in the last 24 hours. She held back a laugh, afraid of waking her. Kat had been right. She liked to make a mess. And here Sadie was, along for the ride, every step of the way. Just like old times. She had that effect. The last time she'd seen Kat she told her she loved her. Did she still? She thought about the video, the way those guys treated Kat. She wanted to kill them. The very thought sent ice to her stomach. Kat shifted, still lying on her, squeezing Sadie tighter. She didn't even know what she was feeling. Despite the mess Todd had gotten Kat in she still felt something close to happy. Some joy in having her back. No matter what that meant. The first months after Kat left had felt like she'd been amputated. Like something vital had been shorn away. For years she felt the phantom pains. Made so much worse by the lack of closure. Kat had been done with her and she set her aside. Maybe Kat had been more like her father than she realized. Now she was here, maybe doing the same thing, and acting the same way. Like before. Like no time had passed. And she wasn't with Jaime anymore. She believed in Kat though. Couldn't help but trust her. Trust she was doing the best she could. The girl she knew never used people. The girl she knew was full of life, and joy, and love. Who was she now?

"Do you want to get under the blanket?" Kat mumbled into her chest.

"Okay," Sadie said, letting the soothing lilt of Kat's voice pull her from her runaway thoughts.

Kat grasped onto the belt loop on Sadie's jeans giving a gentle tug on the fabric. "Are you comfy?" she asked.

"Oh," Sadie chuckled, "I'll change." She extracted herself from Kat's embrace. Kat sat up watching Sadie dig through dresser drawers till she found a suitable pair of shorts and black tank top and disappeared into the bathroom. Kat felt a small pang of remorse at her brief departure. She shut her eyes resting back into the pillows. Everything she was doing was wrong. She should have stayed away from Sadie, kept her out of her shitty messes like she had promised herself years ago. But she was back in the city and scared and alone and like always her first thought had been Sadie. And once she was real Kat couldn't resist her. Sadie felt like home. Instantly. And in all the confusion, the revelation made her shake.

The bathroom door opened and Sadie returned, placing her clothes in a nearby hamper. Kat pulled the blanket down for

Sadie, letting her slip in beside her. Sadie lay still next to her. Kat was too tired to stop herself from pulling Sadie closer till her head was resting against her shoulder, her body pressed against Kat's side. Kat scratched her back through the shirt in soothing strokes till she could feel Sadie's breath even out. Kat matched her own breaths to Sadie's till she drifted off thankful for this moment she stumbled into. The rain fell heavy outside, the low rumble of thunder fading in the distance.

Wrapped in Kat's arms, her touch warming her cold body under the blankets, Sadie felt heavier than she had in a long time. The weight of sleep pressed down on her till everything in her let go.

As sleep set in, Sadie began to fall. She fell deeper and deeper into an ever growing darkness. Falling till she hit rock bottom, colliding into an earthen floor, damp and dusty with age. Her body hit with a thud, her back connecting, disturbing the ancient dust, throwing it into the air in a billowing cloud. Sadie tried to take a breath but the dust only choked her, making her cough in painful fits. Blinking hard, she tried to clear her vision to no avail. The darkness swallowed the whole world. Forcing herself to move, Sadie rolled onto her hands and knees and began to crawl. All she felt was endless dirt. It felt like hours slowly ticked by before her hand brushed against cold metal. The sensation made her senses spark to life, electrifying after their long absence. She picked the object up, quickly recognizing it for what it was. She fumbled with the gun in the dark, till was grasping the pistol tightly between both hands. Her fears only seemed to grow despite the weapon in hand.

A deep rumble echoed through the room, shaking its foundations. Sadie gripped the gun tighter, fighting the sudden nausea that overcame her. A flashing light blinded Sadie, filling the room with its searing brightness. When her vision returned to her she could make out a shaft of light spilling effortlessly from a doorway suddenly thrust open. An ominous shadow cut across the frame. To her right came the sharp sound of a girl crying. Sadie looked over trying to find her, but everything outside the small pillar of light was still an inky pitch black. Turning back to the door Sadie could make out a second figure, smaller, frail and hunched over.

A thunderous cracking sound filled the room, so loud it made Sadie's ears ring. She looked down to her hands no longer cradling the pistol. Instead, they were empty and smeared red with wet, sticky blood, the dirt from the floor caked onto her palms. The shaft of light began to shrink as the door shut, slowly leaving Sadie in the dark once again. With the light gone all the air seemed to drain out of the room, leaving Sadie helplessly gasping for air.

A distant voice broke through the haze of her suffocating mind.

"Sadie?"

Sadie startled awake, heart pounding violently against her ribs, fighting to catch her breath. A crack of lightning painted the world an electric blue before turning gray. The clap of thunder brought her back to reality, staring into Kat's face above her, dimly lit in the darkened room. Kat looked…afraid. A tear trickled from her eye landing on Sadie's cheek. She collected

Sadie in her arms, hugging her tight.

"You looked so scared. You were crying. In your sleep," Kat said, face pressed into Sadie's hair. "Are you okay?"

Sadie pulled away, looking Kat in the eyes, "Just a bad dream."

"I've never seen you...like that," Kat said, her eyebrows knit together, face pinched as she searched Sadie. "What was it about?"

"Something bad that happened. A while ago," Sadie answered, pausing to steady herself. "Three years ago."

Kat's eyes moved back and forth reading the fear on Sadie. She tucked a lock of hair behind her ear, her hand lingering on Sadie's face. "It's okay," she whispered. "You don't have to tell me."

Sadie took her hand from her face, letting it fall between them. "I can...I can." She blinked against the dark. "We were working...I was working a missing person case with Hector. A cold case. A year old." Kat listened patiently, holding onto Sadie's hand, eyes fixated on the other woman. "The parents were really determined. It didn't seem likely, but we found something." Sadie absently continued, looking at the storm clouds out the window. "A girl. Leah. Went missing when she was 11. We found her. In a house. The basement. It seemed abandoned, really. We were trying to get her out when the guy who took her showed up. He blindly shot, hit the girl. Then he ran. Hector stayed with her. Told me not to go after him. I didn't listen." Sadie paused, disappearing somewhere

Kat couldn't follow. Kat squeezed her hand, reminding her she was right beside her, bringing Sadie back to the present. Her eyes refocused and her gaze met Kat's. She blinked back tears. Kat waited. "He managed to corner me. He attacked me, dropped the gun. When he charged at me, I went for it. I shot him. He died. Right in front of me. Leah. She lived. She's different. She can't walk, but she's safe. And with her family."

"You helped her," Kat said.

Sadie didn't look convinced. "You ever seen anyone die?"

"Yes," Kat answered. Sadie's eyebrows raised, surprise marring her features. "He overdosed." Sadie's eyes grew larger. "I wanted to help him, but um," Kat cleared her throat. "I um…" She blinked. "Was overdosing. Someone came and helped me in time. But he took more, I think."

Sadie inched closer, resting her forehead against Kat's."I'm sorry," she whispered.

"It's not your fault," Kat answered. "Is that what you dreamt about?"

"Yeah. It happens sometimes." Sadie toyed with Kat's hand still in hers. "Do you think I'm a bad person?"

Kat's heart ached with the vulnerability laced through her voice. "No," she answered adamantly. Hating the idea of considering Sadie anything less than perfect. "Do you think I'm bad?"

"Never," Sadie was ardent in her answer. There was a hitch in Kat's breathing. She could feel her warm breath against her lips.

"S-Sadie," Kat whispered, looking hopelessly lost. "We should-"

"Eat." Sadie laughed quietly. "I agree. I'm starving." In a swift motion, she was out of bed and gently tugging Kat from the comfortable pile of blankets. Kat followed along willingly, her soft smile filled with quiet relief. The kitchen was small but serviceable. The few items there were neatly arranged. Sadie released Kat's hand. Idling over to the refrigerator, she swung the door open hunting for nourishment. "I'm not exactly sure what I can make work here." She dug through the contents of shelves, tossing items back and forth. Kat leaned against the counter watching the way Sadie's muscles moved subtly, the way her arms looked in her tank top.

"Let me look," Kat said, nudging Sadie aside. The other woman stepped away giving her a little smile. Kat felt her heart clench at how sweet and innocent she looked in that moment.

Sadie turned her attention to a row of nearby cabinets. Opening the wooden doors, the hinges squeaking in protest. "I have noodles."

"What kind?" Kat asked, collecting things from the fridge.

"Elbows, spaghetti."

"I think we're in luck." Kat pulled a carton of milk from the fridge, alongside it some shredded cheese and butter. Placing the items on the counter she continued, "We used to make mac and cheese all the time!" Her smile was enormous, blossoming to light up her whole face.

"That mac n cheese came from a box. So a little different."

"It's easy." Kat wiggled her eyebrows at Sadie.

"Just throw a vegetable or two in there if you can." Sadie's lips quirked with a half smile, catching glimpses of the girl she knew peaking through.

"Vegetables!" Kat laughed. "Very mature. We used to put hot dogs in our macaroni."

"I might have some in the freezer." Sadie plucked the macaroni from the cabinet, adding it to the pile on the counter.

Kat looked up, momentarily lost in thought, like she was investigating her own mind. "I haven't had a hot dog in a very long time." She shook her head, snapping back to reality.

Sadie found a pot in the dishwasher and filled it with water from the tap. Placing it on the stove she turned the knob, listening for the familiar click before the flame. She sprinkled some salt in the water, watching the dots dissolve into nothing. Turning back she saw Kat producing a stalk of broccoli brandishing it playfully in the air.

"Does this work for you?" she asked. Sadie nodded, passing

Kat a cutting board and knife. Kat washed the broccoli before starting her task. As she walked past Sadie noticed black tendrils of tattoo ink peeking out from Kat's shorts. Biting her lip she brought her eyes back to Kat's face, watching her start cutting broccoli neatly.

"I'll be right back," Sadie said. "Do you need anything?"

"I'm good," Kat said watching Sadie leave before browsing the kitchen in search of another pot.

Sadie went to the living room. Finding her jacket she dug out her phone. The screen illuminated. Nothing from Daniel. She sat on the sofa, putting the phone on the coffee table. With a deep sigh she sank into the cushions. She needed a moment alone. All of this was so much. She had no clue what she was going to do. Everything so far had been on instinct. Now Kat was in her kitchen. She'd told her the worst thing that'd ever happened to her. Clearly Kat had been through a lot too. The thought made her heart ache. Then there was the closeness. Like a sharp and painful glimpse into what might have been. Just like back then, she couldn't control herself. Was it selfish of her to take everything Kat gave, not caring about the consequences. Was Kat thinking the same? Sadie felt her stomach tighten in knots. Lying next to Kat had been the most peaceful she felt in a long time. Her thoughts twisted in on themselves keeping her stuck in place till Kat appeared in the doorway.

"Foods almost ready," she said.

Sadie sat up, registering her. "Oh. Sorry. I spaced out."

"Are you sure you're alright?" she asked, taking a step closer before stopping herself.

"It's just a lot," Sadie answered. "Tell me what you're thinking?"

"Even though my dad's a real bastard, I'm still fucking scared for him." Kat sighed. "I'm glad you're here...I can't-I missed you, I thought about you so much. Now you're here. I can't help but...do things I probably shouldn't."

"I know the feeling," Sadie said. She stood up approaching Kat till she was right before her. "I don't mind though." She leaned in, delicately kissing Kat's cheek. "It's just scary. I'll help finish up." Then she left, returning to the kitchen. For a moment Kat lingered thinking over Sadie's words. She followed her into the kitchen, watching Sadie investigate her handiwork.

"What are you thinking?"

"I'm scared for you." Sadie met Kat's gaze. "I..." She paused, carefully considering her next words. "I like having you here. I don't know what to do."

Kat approached her, touching her arm gently. "What do you want?"

Sadie's face turned soft, vulnerable as she looked deep into Kat's eyes. "I want to be close to you." Silence filled the air between them, heavy and laden with years of history.

Kat came closer, collecting Sadie in her arms. "I want that too."

Sadie wrapped her arms around Kat, cradling her close in the warm kitchen. "I'm right here," she whispered.

The oven timer began to buzz, disturbing the moment. Slowly Sadie extracted herself from the embrace, grabbing a nearby pair of oven mitts and donning them, pulling a small casserole dish from the hot oven and setting it on the stove. Kat busied herself with finding plates and a serving spoon.

"Smells good," Sadie said, inhaling deeply.

"Should taste even better," Kat said, gracing Sadie with a breathtaking smile. Together they made plates and found their way back to the living room. Pressed in the side of the room beside a large window was a small folding card table. Sadie sat her plate down before pulling a chair out for Kat, who graciously sat, enjoying the small gesture. Sadie disappeared from the room, soon returning with two glasses of water. She set one in front of Kat who smiled her thanks. Together they sat watching the last remnants of rain drizzle down outside while they ate.

"What do you do?" Sadie broke the silence. Kat looked at her with a raised eyebrow, prompting Sadie to clarify. "For work."

"I do PR," Kat said, setting her cup down. "In L.A."

"That sounds exciting." Sadie gave a wistful smile.

"It's okay," Kat said. "It's fun."

"How long have you been in L.A.?"

"Six years. Give or take," Kat answered, pausing to take a bite. "You know I went to Stanford. I moved right after graduation."

"Do you like it?" Sadie asked earnestly. She felt like she was prying but couldn't resist quelling the endless pool of curiosity.

"I guess." Kat's answer was non-committal as she innocently stared at Sadie. "How about you?"

Sadie's face turned hopelessly confused. "What about me?"

"You own the agency now?" Kat asked. "How'd that happen? I mean you were always hanging around Marissa and Hector growing up."

Sadie smiled at the mention of Daedalus' former owners Detectives Hector and Marissa Reyes. They were like parents to her. Better than her own in any case. "After high school, I started working full-time for them. Doing secretary stuff. They said they'd promote me to junior detective if I took some classes. I think they were just trying to give me something to go after." Sadie paused, looking out the window. "I did well. They took me on. Eventually, they retired and left me the place." Sadie turned back to Kat. "It's been a year now. Today."

Kat's eyebrows raised, eyes widening at the revelation. "Happy Anniversary!" Kat said, touching Sadie's hand in the process.

"I know just the thing." Kat's face broke into an excited grin. She ran out of the living room only to return a moment later. "Cake might be more traditional, but I found this in the fridge." She produced the small container from the cafe and two forks. With a grand gesture, she presented it to Sadie who smiled, graciously taking the box. Kat returned to her seat watching Sadie open the container.

"Here," Sadie said, spearing a small section of the pie and offering it to Kat.

"You should have the first bite." Kat shook her head.

"I insist." Sadie held the fork aloft. Kat rolled her eyes before leaning forward, taking the offered taste. Her eyes met Sadie's as she lingered over the dessert. "Is it good?" Kat pulled away, licking her lips in appreciation.

"Try some," Kat said, using her own fork to offer a bite to the other woman. Sadie gave a mischievous smirk before trying it. "Sadie," Kat said."I missed you."

"I know," Sadie replied, her mind a clash of confusion. They spent the rest of the meal in a peaceful quiet, the sound of trickling rain outside turning the world dreamy. Unsure what to do, they took to the sofa, Sadie casually putting on an old movie, not fully paying attention as she intermittently checked her phone waiting for Daniel. She hoped the video wouldn't frighten him away from helping. Otherwise, she didn't know what to do short of staking out Todd's apartment, maybe the bar. She looked over, taking in Kat, curled up with a fleece blanket, the lights of the tv flickering across her face. The thought of leaving Kat by herself for that long tore her up with worry. The thought of bringing her along was worse, sending an icy chill in the pit of her stomach. Kat turned catching Sadie staring at her. Sadie didn't look away.

"Hey," Kat said, voice quiet. "I'm sorry. That I hurt you so much." She reached out tentatively, taking Sadie's hand. "I don't know if you should forgive me. But I wanted to say it anyway."

Sadie nodded solemnly. Entwining their fingers together, she felt a gentle squeeze in response. "We have a lot to talk about, huh?"

"I know," Kat answered, feeling the weight of acknowledgment. The baggage they had quietly agreed to pile in a corner, forgotten, suddenly brought to light.

"The last time I saw you, you told me you loved me," Sadie said, voice faint. Kat nodded, a quiet and hopeful smile forming on her lips. "And then I didn't see you for ten years." Kat faltered. Sadie gave her hand a gentle squeeze. "I'm not mad. Not anymore. I get why. I just...I wish you didn't disappear."

Kat felt panicked at the pain written on Sadie's face. "I wanted to." She inched closer, relieved when Sadie didn't pull away. "I thought you hated me. I hated me..." She trailed off. With her free hand, Sadie tucked a lock of auburn hair behind Kat's ear. "Jaime knew...how I felt about you. I felt guilty."

"We were 18," Sadie said, playing with Kat's fingers. "Do you need me to forgive you?" The ache in the pit of her stomach had only grown.

"Only if you meant it," Kat answered, her words hanging between them.

"It took me a long time. I loved you. So much." Sadie's brows knit together, her voice cracking. "We made love. You were my... you were my first. Then you just ran off. With that creep."

"She's not a creep," Kat chimed in, voice oddly even. Sadie didn't seem convinced. "It's complicated," she sighed. "But it's over."

"You never said anything. I didn't know where you were."

"I didn't know what to say," Kat answered.

"And now?" Sadie asked, taking in the ocean of Kat's eyes, unsure of what she was doing, the rift that question might cause.

"I thought about you. Everyday. Even when I tried not to. I was scared and I took the only way out I saw. I didn't-" She paused, taking a deep breath. "I didn't think you loved me. Didn't think I deserved you. And all that awful stuff back home. I couldn't-" Kat choked. "I couldn't stay."

"I know," Sadie took Kat in her arms. "I told you I get it. I forgive you," she whispered. "I'm glad it was you. I wouldn't change that."

Kat pulled away, just enough to cup Sadie's cheek. "You were my first love, y'know." The pair became caught in a trance, the room filling with silence till Kat couldn't take it, and against any shred of reason she asked. "Can I kiss you?" Sadie nodded subtly. Kat drifted closer till her lips met Sadie's and that overwhelming ache gave way to some semblance of relief that seemed to recede and transform into a deep yearning till the crush of Kat's lips silenced it again. The echoes of that long absence flooded their kisses, shadowing each movement. Sadie grasped onto her afraid she might drift away, unconsciously pulling till Kat was on top of her, cradled in Sadie's lap while she kissed Sadie over and over again, scarcely breathing between. "I still want you." Kat's voice was low, a warm breath against Sadie's ear.

Sadie bit back a moan, pulling Kat close again, kissing her passionately. "I never stopped wanting you."

She sighed against Kat's mouth. At her words Kat's hands slid under the hem of her shirt, running along her stomach and sides. And just like the first time she felt drunk on her, overwhelmed, and completely lost to Kat. She kissed her hard, memorizing the way she felt as she grasped onto her sides, pulling her in.

"Are you sure?" Kat asked.

"Yes," Sadie's voice was husky. She kissed Kat again, one hand tangled in her hair, the other at her hip. Kat bit her lip, licking it carefully after. "Come with me," she whispered, setting aside the millions of things she wanted to say, lifting Kat off the sofa. Taking Kat by the hand she led her to the bedroom. Kat followed helplessly.

They returned to the darkened bedroom, Sadie sitting on the crumpled blankets they had left behind. Kat stood between her legs looking down at the other woman. Sadie leaned back to meet Kat's gaze, she tentatively ran a hand from Kat's cheek to her neck and down her side. Kat moaned, leaning in to kiss Sadie's neck, her warm breath tickling the skin there. Her lips traced Sadie's neck to her jaw until she found her lips again. She ran her tongue gently across Sadie's lower lip before kissing her softly, slowly, searing her passion into her. She climbed on top of Sadie, feeling her hips between her thighs as she forced Sadie onto her back, still kissing every piece of available skin.

The rain began to pour heavier outside, a torrential downpour, only broken up by lightning and echoing claps of thunder, punctuating their frantic movements, desperately trying to get closer to one another. It seemed like hours before they reemerged from their fervor, both sated, bodies humming with ripples of pleasure, their breathing frantic but slowly quieting to normal as they met each other's eyes. Sadie kissed Kat tenderly. Kat could feel the trail of wetness against her thigh. Wrapping her arms around Sadie she cradled her close till they were lying breast to breast, Kat's legs wrapped tight against Sadie's hips, keeping her in place. Their panting evened out as they lay in the afterglow, sticky with sweat. Sadie looked Kat in the eye unable to find words. Instead, she kissed Kat with a slow-burning passion, thoroughly exploring her, prolonging the high. When she pulled away she looked and met those familiar eyes once more. Kat tucked a lock of dark hair behind Sadie's ear, staring at her in awe. Sadie began to trace along Kat's hip and thigh where she had first noticed the swirls of ink.

"Tell me about this?" Sadie asked, looking down to get an unobscured look. Etched into Kat's hip was a tree, its branches grasping upwards, its long roots twisted and tangled below, the ink crisscrossing along stretch marks on her thigh.

"Do you remember my Grandma Rosenblum? She adored you. Called you a little guardian angel." Kat stroked Sadie's cheek. Sadie nodded, encouraging her to continue. "Whenever she'd visit before she'd passed, we'd walk to the synagogue she preferred and she'd tell me about this tree called the Tree of Life. When I was in college I read that there was a real Tree of Life. In Bahrain. It doesn't rain there. Not really. The Tree of Life is the only tree for miles, in a place with no water. They say it's 400 years old and no one knows how it survives. When I graduated I went. It was the most surreal experience. This desolate landscape, the melting heat, and this ancient tree refusing to die."

Sadie searched her face, enamored with the girl beneath her. She kissed her cheek before finding her lips, kissing her again and again hopelessly lost to the sensation. Kat met her kiss adding a fierceness that inflamed her. Slowly she began rocking her hips against Kat lost to long buried feelings rising to the surface. Kat thrust back matching her rhythm till they grew lost in one another. Kat wrapped arms around her and with a gentle tug flipped Sadie over so she was beneath her. Kat's kisses began to stray from lips to jaw to chest till she arrived at her chest, kissing each breast in turn, taking care not to miss any spots. Sadie felt the warmth of her mouth burning into her, felt the fire Kat seemed intent to brand her with. Her kisses strayed further across her ribcage, her stomach till she reached her hips, splaying tender kisses and gentle bites everywhere, delicately worshiping Sadie. She reached the tops of Sadie's thighs kissing all over before finding where they met. She took her time in her worship, loving Sadie, feeling the sway of her hips beneath her, the taste of her overwhelming her senses and drawing her deeper in. She reached a hand out taking Sadie's, entwining their fingers, listening to the soft keening moans and gasps as she loved her. Soon Sadie gasped, squeezing Kat's hand as she peeked under Kat's touch. Kat came up, collecting Sadie in her arms, wrapping the blanket around them. Still trembling in the aftershock Sadie kissed Kat's soft lips, she drifted to sleep feeling possessed by Kat, lost to her all over again.

Sadie woke to the persistent hum of her phone ringing from the other room. She was under the covers, Kat clinging to her, her naked body pressed into her. It was completely dark outside. Save for the flicker of street lamps filtering through the window. Carefully Sadie extracted herself, making sure Kat was still covered by the blanket. She found the phone abandoned and buzzing on the coffee table. Quickly she silenced it, answering to hear Daniel's voice on the other end.

"Sadie!" He greeted though notably less chipper than normal. "I got the info you wanted. Meet me at the cafe. In 20 minutes."

"Okay," she answered. He scarcely gave her time to speak before hanging up. Sadie snuck back into the bedroom taking care not to jar the woman sleeping in her bed. Shaking her shoulder Sadie woke Kat. "Hey," she whispered, "Daniel has intel for us. About your dad." Kat sat up at the words. "No-no. You can go back to sleep. I won't be long. Will you be okay?"

"Yeah." Kat nodded, eyes wide as she tried to absorb the information. "Find out, okay? But hurry back." Kat asked, so vulnerable it made Sadie's heartache. She kissed Kat, not hesitating as she embraced her.

"I won't be long," Sadie promised, kissing her again before dressing quickly.

"Sadie," Kat said, eyes lingering on Sadie as she prepared to go. "Why are you helping me?"

"I…" Sadie started before drifting off, halting in her task. She turned to gaze at Kat still nestled in her bed. "You never met my mom. She died before we ever knew each other." Kat nodded, remembering the somber cloud of that absence that had followed her friend since they were kids. "Except she didn't."

"What?" Kat sat up, mouth falling open. "What do you mean?"

"After you left. I looked into it. My dad said she died, but… but we never had a funeral, I never even knew what happened. Was she sick? Was there an accident?" Sadie sighed, sitting on the edge of the bed where she began to lace up her shoes. Trying to fixate on the task at hand. "Hector and Marissa helped me look. They said there was never a death certificate issued. As close as they can tell, she just left one day. If I could...I would give anything to see her again and just find out. Y'know? Find out why," Sadie's voice cracked as she spoke, her eyes were wet, but the tears refused to fall. "If I can't have that chance, at least you can get yours."

Kat sat up moving closer to Sadie's frozen form. With a gentle hand, she turned Sadie's face to look at her, wanting to see her face. She kissed her temple, pulling her closer till she was encased in her arms. Sadie sank into the embrace, drawing courage from Kat. Sadie pulled away just enough to kiss Kat's lips before letting go.

"I'm sorry," Kat said, reluctant to let Sadie out of her arms.

"It's okay," Sadie answered. "I have to leave."

Kat watched each movement as Sadie finished putting herself in order, savoring the sight of her, the personal intimate ways she did things, wondering at all these new scars Sadie had acquired in those long, absent years. Her eyes remained fixated til the final traces of Sadie disappeared out the door. She lay back in the bed, suddenly wide awake and staring into an unfamiliar ceiling in a darkened bedroom, street light filtering in through the windows. Turning on her side she reached out for Sadie's pillow hugging it close to her chest, inhaling the scent of *her.* The world had turned so chaotic and still, Sadie seemed to be her oasis. She hadn't intended for any of this to happen. But despite all her worry and maybe because of it she had crash-landed into Sadie's life, her arms, and now her bed. And it had felt as good as she always thought it would. Of course, now there was a mess of confusion to figure out. Like would she stay in Sadie's life now they were reunited? After they found her dad, what then? Kat sighed into the pillow, turning over, pillow still close like a shield against her thundering thoughts.

Her eyes were adjusting and in her newfound understanding of the darkness, she scanned the little things on Sadie's nightstand. The old lamp, an analog alarm clock with no lights, a takeout container, some papers. She puzzled together ideas of Sadie's daily life. The quiet, private moments that seem so inconsequential. Reaching a hand out she touched the papers, noticing the slick gloss surface. Photo paper. Kat pulled the stack closer investigating the images. She reached for the lamp's switch, fumbling a moment till she figured out the button. With a click, a small pool of light spilled forth. Kat came face to face with a vision from the past. Caught within the frame, her and Sadie, maybe 15 years old. She couldn't remember the exact moment taking place, she recalled the feeling though. She had only started realizing why she never cared for the boys that chased after her attention. Tangled in that revelation was the newfound understanding of burgeoning feelings for her lifelong best friend. Mixed in with the flush of first love and teenage excitement was the abject fear that Sadie could never feel the same, that her best friend would turn to her with disgust, would look at her in hate. The thought tore her apart. She started having nightmares about it. Interspersed with a myriad of confusing dreams, often featuring Sadie.

She flipped to the next photograph. Another image of herself was looking back. 13 this time, standing in front of a shop window, Sadie's reflection caught in the glass next to her, camera pressed to her face, obscuring her, a tangle of black hair surrounding the device, seemingly swaying in the wind. It wasn't long after Sadie met the Reyes's. Marissa had seemed taken with Sadie's wily, rough around the edges way and gifted her the camera. Along with photos of strangers on the streets and buildings and clouds, Sadie had taken to capturing Kat's image.

The next photo was from junior prom. Afterward from what she could tell. A group photo with their high school friends outside the school. Like always Kat was standing next to Sadie. She was wrapped in her jacket to fend off the nighttime chill. Sadie's arm casually slung around her shoulder, huddled close. She wondered if Sadie had any concept of the butterflies she had given her. In the harsh light of hindsight, she realized that maybe she had. In her own way. Kat's life had already started to sift all around her. The first rifts between her and Sadie started to appear. Because of the things she kept hidden from her best friend who she loved so much. Prom had been a welcome reprieve. They had decided to go together. Sadie had found her after school like normal only this time she asked her to prom. As friends. Something she scrambled to explain, going on that Billy Jenkins had been pestering her to go with him and all she really wanted was to spend the night with her best friend. In a way it warmed Kat's heart. Sadie said she understood if she was already Manny Flores's date. Kat said she wasn't. The result filled her with a rush of guilty excitement. But this one indulgence couldn't hurt. They were going as friends. Sadie didn't love her. And she convinced herself that it didn't have to matter.

Kat moved on to the next photograph. At the diner after prom. Sadie was behind Kat, arms around her, embracing her. Kat's face was completely flush in the image. The memory began to trickle back to her. She was pretty drunk at that point in the night. She had bumped into Manny Flores at prom. He was big and handsome and popular. He had asked her to prom the day before Sadie asked. She never told Sadie that though. Manny saw them together and, finding themselves in a private moment, Manny had asked if Sadie was her date. In a flurry of drunken words, he went on about how he thought that was cool, that they made a cute couple. Then he shoved a flask in her direction. She thanked him as he stumbled off. She shared the whiskey with Sadie that night, both of them becoming flush with the unfamiliar warmth. Kat had decided then to embrace the night. To selfishly take what she had spent so long secretly wanting. Before they left that night they had slow danced, swaying together on the darkened floor, forgetting about all the people surrounding them.

At the diner Kat had sat next to Sadie in their large booth, so close she was practically sitting on Sadie's lap. She leaned into her whenever she could, catching wisps of her scent, the warmth of her body. Her heart ached painfully and in that youthful moment everything unraveled for her. Looking up past the sea of friends and acquaintances flooding the diner was a familiar face, out of place in this world. Jaime. Jaime who she had secretly been seeing for half a year, though labels had seemed to elude the romance they had become entangled in. Jaime who was cool, and smart, and rich, with her own apartment and so much of what Kat wanted to be. The older woman was staring quietly across the room, face pinched, scrutinizing every detail of what she was seeing. Kat had felt sick to her stomach, the world spinning as she realized she'd be answering for a lot very soon.

She had met Jaime at an art museum. Feeling frustrated with something or other she had decided to skip school. It wasn't like her absentee mother would ever notice. There had been a heat wave and the museum was frigidly cold. She moved from room to room, lingering over her favorite pieces. In a room tucked off to the side she found herself entranced by a painting of a woman, half-naked, caught mid-twirl, dancing across the canvas, face contorted in joy. She stared so long she didn't notice Jaime materialize beside her. Moments passed by before suddenly she noticed her, with her long blonde hair, warm eyes that seemed lonely, sad and delicate features set in a broad face. Kat told her the woman was beautiful because she was free. Jaime said she envied her.

They explored the rest of the museum together never speaking about themselves till Jaime had invited her to dinner. She'd never been asked to dinner by a beautiful, charming woman before. It couldn't hurt to indulge her fantasies for one night. Dinner was when Jaime asked her what she did for a living and Kat was suddenly dumbstruck. She said she was a student.

Jaime assumed college. Kat agreed, changing the subject. It made a little sense. In those days the only ways she had access to money was doing homework for kids and buying cigarettes and beer for other kids. She had developed quickly growing up and she quickly realized with the right smile and words strangers were apt to believe what they wanted. Jaime seemed to be the same. It was the first time Kat didn't mind. She had touched Jaime's hand, leaned in, and asked her all about herself. Jaime said she was recently divorced, from a man her family had loved. She said she had tried to be what they wanted but she couldn't stay with someone she didn't love. Kat told her it was funny how something that came so natural was so painfully complicated.

That was the beginning of a very long affair.

That night, after prom, Jaime realized the lie. Kat didn't go after her. Jaime didn't approach. Didn't make a scene. That was never her style. Sadie noticed the sudden shift, had looked right at Jaime staring at them cuddled together in the diner booth, Kat still in Sadie's jacket. Sadie had turned and kissed her temple, lingering a moment there. Kat blushed, resisting pulling away, feeling her stomach drop under Jaime's gaze. Jaime only walked away, briefly speaking to the group she came with before disappearing. Kat stayed the night with Sadie, falling asleep together in her bed, entangled, still dressed in their fancy clothes. Tomorrow she would face the music. Tonight was for pretend.

She went to Jaime the next day. It had been awful. Jaime looked so betrayed. Until then Kat hadn't fully grasped how much she loved Jaime, not till the thought of never seeing her again became real. Jaime had told her how much she cared for her but she couldn't see her anymore. Kat cried in Jaime's arms at the revelation. Jaime called her a car. When she stumbled out of the expensive black sedan outside her shabby apartment building Sadie was there, almost like she had been waiting. Kat had been intent on going to her apartment where her mother would ignore her while she cried about getting dumped. Instead, Sadie was asking her where she'd been. Sadie looked so upset. Her heart ached so much, she couldn't take anymore. Sadie wanted to talk. She told her she couldn't. She left her standing there.

She didn't speak to Jaime or Sadie for weeks. The school year ended and she was alone and heartbroken. And for the first time in her young life she didn't feel like she could go to her best friend. In the early weeks of that summer her mother told her that Uncle Tommy was getting out of jail, that he'd be staying with them. Tommy terrified her. He'd lived with them before, not long after her dad had gone for good. At first he was nice. Loving. Doting. The thing she thought a good parent might be. Then he grew frightening. The ways he lingered over her, touched her when he shouldn't. It made her not like him anymore. She had been too young to articulate it. In any case, her mother didn't believe her clumsy explanation. It had been a small miracle that he'd gotten picked up on a car theft warrant. Even better that he'd tried to fist fight the cop. Now he was back and Kat was not just alone, she was scared.

She had gone to the only person she knew could help her. Jaime. And she had. It was messy and complicated, but she let her stay. She gave her a room, told her she'd get her into a better school in the fall. Only for the school year, till she could get into college. Kat ran home to tell Sadie, forgetting the awkwardness they had left off on.

When Sadie had opened her apartment door she looked exhausted, drawn, with huge bags under her eyes. She'd never seen a sight like it. She reached for her, touching her arms, pulling her into a hug. Sadie pushed her away. Kat swallowed back the instant swell of tears. Sadie had never treated her that way. In her sad, quiet voice she asked what she wanted. Kat told her she was sorry. Sadie shook her head asking again. Kat told her she'd be leaving. That Tommy was coming back, that Jaime said she could stay. Sadie cried as her story unfolded. When she started to speak she went on about how she was abandoning her for Jaime, that she wasn't good enough. Kat told her it was different. That Jaime loved her. Sadie touched her then, pulling her close, telling her she loved her. Everything in Kat shut down. Her body went on autopilot and suddenly she was kissing Sadie for the first time. She felt like she was imploding, like somehow she'd slipped out of the universe, the only other person surviving, Sadie. She'd stayed the night with her and they talked. About everything. In the early morning hours as the sun drifted through the windows, she lay holding Sadie realizing the immense weight of hiding so much from her for so long.

Kat laughed to herself, setting the photos down on the nightstand. Now, as then, being back with Sadie somehow felt like breathing again. Like the relief of coming home after a long trip. She didn't deserve it. For a moment she began to cry, shedding the weight of everything. What was she going to do when all the madness was over? When she left again?

In the hushed quiet of the small apartment, the sound of someone at the door broke Kat's meandering thoughts. She sat up, hurriedly wiping tears from her face.

"Sadie?"

Five blocks away Sadie paced back and forth outside a 24 hour diner waiting for Daniel. He hadn't been inside and she hardly felt like waiting idly. She wanted to get home. She felt the prickly sensation of fear mixing with the wet cold the night had taken on. It sent a chill straight to her bones. A hot shower sounded good. Her thoughts drifted to Kat in her bed. The world felt out of control and she had no idea what to do. Protecting Kat was enough for now. After all this she'd figure the rest out. Sadie forced herself to stop the pacing, instead watching her breath mist in the air, catching in the light of street lamps before drifting away. Shaking her head she wondered why she was so eager to slip into the fantasy with Kat. Sadie told herself to accept whatever it was, as is, before Kat slipped away again.

Across the street a car approached, its headlights cutting through the night. It came to an abrupt halt at Sadie's feet. Peering through the passenger window she caught Daniel's silhouette behind the wheel, the street lights glittering against lingering droplets across the windshield, creating little droplets of cascading light across Daniel's face. Sadie grasped the door handle, pulling it open and slipping inside away from the chill.

"What took you so long?" Sadie asked only half serious. Daniel only held a file folder between them.

"It's really hard for me to want to give this to you," Daniel said. "Your client should press charges."

"Against mobster goons?" Sadie asked.

"So we can help," Daniel answered, placing the folder on the dashboard. It looked tattered and stuffed with too many papers.

"You are helping," Sadie said.

"And what happens when you find these guys?"

"I'm not looking for them. I'm looking for Todd."

"Sounds like the same thing," Daniel said, eyes lingering on the file.

"What do you want me to do?" Sadie asked, the lights of passing cars illuminated Daniel in bursts.

"Look, these guys are into some bad shit," Daniel said. "And they're already getting aggressive."

"I'm not gonna do anything," Sadie said, fighting to keep the irritation out of her voice. "I'm just trying to help Kat. That's it."

Daniel searched her face for a long, silent moment. "You're gonna get her hurt," he said, quiet voice filling the car.

"Well she's not backing down from this," Sadie answered. "All I can do is try to protect her."

Daniel grasped the file holding it in front of himself. "You have to call me at the first sign of trouble. And when you call you have to tell me the truth."

"Okay." Sadie nodded. "I promise."

Daniel scrutinized her for a moment more before reluctantly handing the file over. "I'm going home. I'm trusting you," Daniel said, eyebrows pinched together.

"Thank you." Sadie got out of the car and with scarcely a look back Daniel was gone, disappearing into the night.

She clutched the file tight, all but sprinting back to her apartment, panting against the cold, heart aching in her rib cage. The labyrinth of quiet city streets gave way to Sadie's apartment building. Pulling the door open too hard she ran through the door and hurriedly began her climb up the stairs, eager to be back with Kat. Reaching the landing she caught sight of her apartment door left slightly ajar. Sadie's eyes grew large, dark eyebrows knit together in cautious fear.

She slowed her pace, fighting against her instinct to charge inside. Moving as quietly as she could on the rickety wooden floor, silencing the thoughts in her head, she strained to listen through the crack in the door. The lock hung awkwardly, the door jam splintered from force. She eased the door open inching her way inside the darkened apartment. The place was eerily silent. The floor was covered with papers and overturned items. She tiptoed further in scanning the room for something to use as a weapon. She kept a baseball bat under her bed for shit like this. Against the silence, she heard subtle shifting, a muffled groan. From the living room, she caught the barest glimpse of Kat, wrapped in the fierce grip of the hooked nose man, one of his meaty hands clamped over Kat's mouth. Kat struggled against him. He had a gash across one eye, bleeding freely down his cheek. Sadie stepped towards the bedroom then stopped, her feet suddenly unable to move. She was falling fast, a sharp, jarring pain hot and fast flooding her vision in white, blotting out the world, making her ears ring. The white faded as she crumpled to the floor, head bouncing off the hardwood. Everything going black as she slipped away.

Chapter Three

The world was possessed of a sharp splitting.

A shrill sound echoed, redoubling the searing pain.

Sadie's eyes slid open only to retreat again fighting a wave of nausea. Her head felt cracked open. Nearby was her baseball bat, half smeared in her blood, still wet and dripping onto the carpet. Slowly she felt her head, investigating the damage. Shockwaves of pain echoed out where her hand touched, coming away with traces of sticky blood, red against her fingertips. With one hand on the floor, Sadie pushed herself up from the ground slipping as she tried to right herself. Under her palm were scattered papers, newly smeared with her bloody fingerprints. In her bleary daze, Sadie made out the file folder on the floor not far from her. They must have been in a hurry. Clutching her head she stood, letting the world stop spinning before she collected the myriad of papers off the floor, tucking them back into the folder, fighting another wave of nausea. Stumbling she pressed her back into the wall, using it to anchor herself. Breathing deeply Sadie blindly dug for her phone, pulling it from her pocket. Pressing buttons, the screen lit up casting a bright glow in the darkened room. The light cut into Sadie's throbbing skull. Forcing herself to dial. After long moments of endless ringing, the line finally connected.

"D-Daniel?" Sadie said, voice trembling as she connected jumbled strings of sentences in her head. "The guys. Th-they broke into my apartment. They kidnapped Kat. I need you."

"Sadie?" Daniel asked, voice hazy with sleep. "Are you okay?"

"Absolutely not," Sadie answered. "I need you to get here. With cops. Find out where they took her."

"I'll be right there. Don't go anywhere." Daniel sounded more awake. Sadie hung up without another word.

Clutching her head she slowly pushed herself from the wall stumbling slightly. Through the small living room windows the sky lightened from inky black to gray. In the dark Sadie found a lamp that managed to avoid the mayhem. Shutting her eyes she braced herself, flooding the room in the warm glow of the unbroken bulb. Flipping the file open she scanned the first page. The bald one was named Vincent. There was a listed address attached. The hook-nosed man's name was James, commonly called Jimmy. Another address. Between the set they'd wracked up a number of charges. Petty theft led to drug deals and grand theft auto till they got some attention from their local criminal organization. Daniel said they were small time. New guys. Maybe the $80 grand Todd asked to borrow from Kat was for the mob. Maybe these two were the collection agency. She had to find them. Had to find Todd. He was key to this clusterfuck. Thoughts pounded through Sadie's throbbing head as she frantically pieced together a story, a trail, something she could follow. The file listed some of their usual haunts. A bar, a pool hall, a dog track. She doubted they'd take their hostage to any of those places. Kat was what? Leverage to get Todd, who clearly wanted to jump ship. He didn't even know Kat was in the city. Was he even in the city?

Outside the window blue and red flashing lights illuminated the streets, cascading into the apartment. Through the open door came the echo of hurried footsteps up wooden steps. Daniel came running into the cramped apartment, spotting Sadie immediately. Moments later a couple uniformed officers ran in behind him. A wave of pain washed through Sadie sending the room spinning. She stumbled into Daniel feeling faint against the swirl of confusion. Daniel eased her onto the nearby sofa giving her a moment to collect herself, instructing the cops to search the place for clues. Sadie slid the file under the cushion where she sat.

"I need you to tell me everything, Sadie," Daniel said, voice preternaturally quiet.

"The guys from the video were here when I got back. They took Kat. You need to help me find her."

"What's her full name?" Daniel asked. "Do you have a photo of her?"

Sadie nodded, pulling out her phone and sending Daniel a photo. "Katherine Paige Everett. She's Todd Everett's kid. I'm guessing she's bait for Todd." Sadie clutched her head.

"You need to see a doctor," Daniel said, kneeling in front of her.

"I need to save my friend," Sadie mumbled, vision blurry, scarcely able to focus her eyes on Daniel at her side.

"This is serious shit you're dealing with." He searched her face, his warm eyes tired but inquisitive. "We're going to find her. Why do they want Todd?"

"He owes money. A lot of it. To whoever these guys work for," Sadie said. "Am I being detained?"

"No."

"Find her." Sadie stood pulling the folder from its hiding spot and tucking it under one arm. "I gotta go. Call me if whatever."

"I need you to file a report."

"I'll find you later," Sadie said, slipping out the doorway. She maneuvered the stairs as best she could hoping Daniel wasn't right about going to the hospital.

The morning air outside cleared her head. She navigated the city on autopilot formulating a plan, scarcely noticing the buzzing world around her, or the strange glances from passersby. Sadie found her way to Daedalus Detective Agency fumbling with the lock and falling inside, locking the door behind her. Hurrying to her desk she slid open the bottom drawer producing a small box. Taking a key from her pocket she unlocked the case. Inlaid inside was a small pistol. With a deep breath, she grasped the weapon, feeling the cold metal against her overheated skin. The sensation snapped her into some semblance of reality. She tucked the gun into her waistband before wiping tears from her face.

The world felt quiet for the first time in days.

Sadie went to the bathroom and in the dark fumbled for the light. The fluorescent bulb flickered to life bathing the little cubicle in light. In the mirror was Sadie's reflection, black hair a tangled mess, red blood drying across her forehead and cheek, face starting to swell. She turned the faucet on. The hot water ran till steam began filling the mirror before her face. Slowly she shed her jacket letting it fall to the floor. With both hands cupped together, Sadie collected water and gently splashed it on her face, washing sweat, and blood, and tears away in a swirl down the drain. Blindly she reached for a towel wiping the droplets of water, feeling the remaining few dripping down her chin and neck, disappearing down her shirt. Opening the cabinet she grasped a bottle of aspirin, shaking a few out, and swallowing them with another handful of tepid water. Grabbing the jacket from the floor she ran back out stopping to collect the file on the way

Back on the street, Sadie hailed a cab. From the backseat, she spread the folder open on her lap scanning the page till she found the first address. James's place.

"Can you get me to 8415 West Covington?" She gave the driver the address, closing the folder and leaning back into the headrest. The driver's low music filled the quiet of the cab as the city smeared together outside the glass. The vehicle came to a stop outside a seemingly abandoned building. Sadie got out handing the driver some crumpled bills through the open passenger window before he was off.

The building was desolate. The front door donned an eviction notice with an enormous padlock chained to the door barring entrance. The windows were nailed shut with large sheets of plywood, swirls of graffiti covered every inch of the rotten wood turning it vibrant. From the front it was inaccessible. Sadie circled the building. Patches of overgrown grass clung around the sides of the building, the gutters were collapsed half hanging off in erratic angles. Behind the house were more boarded-up windows and a door. This one with 2 x 4s nailed across. To the edge of the house was a set of concrete stairs leading down to a metal door. Sadie looked around making sure no one was close before descending.

"This is how horror movies start," she whispered to herself.

The door was half rusted but the lock seemed plenty functional. Giving a firm tug it refused to budge. From her jacket pocket, she pulled out a small cloth pouch, nestled inside was a lockpick set. Jamming the needle in Sadie finessed the latch with subtle maneuvers till it gave a satisfying click. She eased the door open, listening intently, hearing nothing. Inside was cold and damp, the basement ridden with a mildewed odor, filled with piles of clutter long discarded, everything covered in thick layers of dust and cobwebs. Sadie carefully inched along the narrow, half-hidden path winding across the room.

Cut into the opposite wall was another stairwell, with splintering wooden stairs and steps that looked liable to disintegrate. Sadie carefully climbed the first stair, hesitating to put her weight on the molded wood. When it held steady she continued up to the wooden door and with her palm pushed it. Her ears strained in the eerie quiet, listening intently for signs of life. The door opened easily. On the other side was a darkened room, mostly empty aside from a couple of folding chairs, a few milk crates overturned to be makeshift tables. One crate held an old television set mounted on top. Empty beer cans and food containers littered the floor. Sadie nudged one of the containers with the toe of her shoe. Inside were rotten, molded remains of food. A roach came scurrying out, hurriedly avoiding Sadie's foot. Piled on top of the crates was a stack of magazines, on the cover were photos of women half naked, breasts spilling out of their shirts, and a layer of dust covering them. Tucked in a corner was a stained mattress. Someone's been here, but not recently. Sadie navigated the abandoned house methodically, room to dusty room, discovering nothing.

In the nascent living room, Sadie laid the folder out on a milk crate turning the pages for the next address, sitting on the edge of a chair, leg bouncing while she read in the dim room. The next lead looked to be several miles away. From upstairs she caught the faint sounds of shuffling followed by a loud clatter, something heavy falling onto wood, muffled through the floor. A spray of dust cascaded from the ceiling across the file folder. She leaned back, tilting her head to look up.

Sadie quietly inched her way up the stairs and down the hallway to where she thought the sound came from. She hung close to the wall moving slowly till she could peer through the open doorway to what might have been a bedroom in a former life. A person in dark clothing lay stretched out on the floor. Their frame was slight and lean, clothes tattered and torn. Whoever they were, they were too small to be who she was looking for. Knocking on the rotting door she made herself known. The person sat up in a hurry.

"Who's there?" came a man's voice, scratchy and irritated.

Sadie inched around the corner, hands in the air and visible. "Hey. I was looking for someone. I don't mean any trouble." The guy nodded, eyeing her up and down. "Have you seen anyone here? Two big guys, one bald."

For long moments the man was silent. Sadie reached into her pocket slow and deliberate, pulling out her wallet, and producing a $20 bill. She walked closer, passing it to the man.

"I've seen guys like that in the neighborhood. But not in the last few weeks. One's got a nose looks like it's been broken half a dozen times?"

Sadie nodded. "I would be careful if they come back here. They're bad guys."

"They're all bad guys," the man said, tucking the bill in his sock.

"If you see them, can you call me?" Sadie asked, kneeling down and passing him her card. "There's a couple hundred bucks in it for you."

The guy took the card looking over the inscription. "There was another guy with them a lot." He tucked the card in his pocket. "Redish hair, smaller, older. Didn't seem like he belonged."

"Have you seen that guy around lately?" Sadie asked, looking him in the eyes.

"No." The guy shook his head. "Sorry. Can I have another dollar?"

Sadie pulled a $10 from her wallet handing it to him. "Thank you," she said. "Please call. And stay safe."

She disappeared out the room collecting the file on her way back out the basement door. Dialing her phone she called for a cab to meet her at the closest major road. Jogging to the road as best she could while digging through her pockets, finding a packet of aspirin, Tearing two out the foil she dry swallowed them. From down the street she could make out the yellow taxi coming to a halt. Sadie ran diving into the back seat and giving the address. The driver didn't talk and through the hazy blur of the ride, jockeying through traffic, Sadie caught snippets on the radio, the news reports endless drone.

"Explosion at the docks...police investigating...no suspect... reward for information leading to an arrest..."

Sadie sighed, staring out the window, taking a moment to wonder about Kat. If she was okay. They wouldn't hurt her if she was a hostage. She wanted to bury the gnawing fear that had been lapping at the edges of her brain. She felt teetering on an edge, wanting to cry and scream. Sadie ached inside, wishing Kat were in the backseat next to her. In her blur of frenzied thoughts she could envision her, her auburn hair in the sunlight, the warm feel of her fingers entwined with her own, the gentle way her thumb would rub the back of her hand in soothing circles, the way Kat would quietly slide across the bench till her leg was pressed against Sadie, resting her head against Sadie's shoulder. She'd say, *It's gonna be okay, I promise.'* Sadie could almost smell her, almost feel the warmth and weight of her body.

"Are you okay, lady?" The driver asked over his shoulder. The car was stopped in front of a run down apartment building. Sadie shook her head, disappearing from her fantasy.

"Yeah. Thank you," she said, passing him his fare before getting out. The cabbie stared after her, lingering to watch her look over the old apartment building before pressing every apartment buzzer but one. The driver shook his head before pulling away from the curb, leaving Sadie behind him.

Sadie listened intently at the buzzer, one hand resting on the door handle. Finally, the tinny sound of buzzing resonated from the busted speaker. She pulled the door, thankful it came open when she did. The file had said apartment 6. The rickety stairs were laid out in an oblong spiral, a wooden railing painted black at its center. Sadie climbed the stairs two at a time, quickly reaching a wooden door with a metallic '6' affixed to it above a peephole. Pressing her ear to the wood she listened for movement, a tv, anything. It was quiet through the thin hollow door. Looking around she stared at the neighbor's door across the hallway. The faint sound of voices in the hall below drifted up. To her left, she could see the stairs continuing up in their curved spiral. She peeked over the railing seeing the backs of two people leaning against the wooden perch talking leisurely. Sadie walked up the stairs climbing each landing till she came to one solitary door at the end of the staircase. Pushing against the metallic door it opened giving way to the rooftop. From above Sadie could see the skyline littered with buildings, checkered with windows, filled with people going about their lives, trapped inside their little bubbles. Surveying the edge of the building she saw a metal ladder protruding off the side. Folding the file in half she tucked it into her pants, glancing over the edge. With a sigh and shake of her head she began climbing down till she reached the first landing and peered in the window making sure no one saw her.

Reconstructing the building in her head she climbed down the fire escape, floor after floor till she reached what she desperately hoped was the right apartment. Making sure the coast was clear Sadie pushed and pulled on the window pane feeling it give way with ease.

"Thank fuck," Sadie said under her breath. She ducked inside through the open window, careful to avoid hitting her still aching head. Her feet touched down on wooden floor. The apartment was still, quiet and lifeless. On a nearby table was a stack of discarded mail. Picking up an envelope she read the name, 'Vincent Madoff', and the apartment address. This was the place. The apartment had been visited not that long ago based on the cold cup of coffee on the coffee table, the sports section of the newspaper laid out alongside it. The paper was three days old. No telling just how long old Vince had been gone. She began searching, combing the apartment for clues. Anything that could point her to where they were hiding Kat. She felt a sudden wave of tangled emotions wash through her at the thought of the other woman. Pausing in her frantic search, she took a steadying breath, letting a tear slide down her cheek. All she wanted was to find Kat and she had no idea what she was doing.

From across the room, the door knob turned, groaned faintly with the movement. Sadie ducked around a corner, tucking tight against a wall in the nearby hallway. Instinctually she reached one hand to her gun, freeing it from her waistband. The door clicked shut. Light footsteps creaked against the floor. Slowly Sadie peered around the corner, crouching low to stay out of sight. She caught glimpses of a jacket, a shoulder. A man's frame. Leaning further out to see, she saw short auburn hair, flecks of gray sprinkling throughout. Sadie watched him shuffle around the living room opening drawers and cabinets, overturning sofa cushions. She stood from her hiding spot, gun still in hand, stepping out of the hallway.

"Todd!"

Todd turned suddenly to face Sadie, surprise making him jump backwards, tripping over the coffee table and collapsing to the floor in a mass of flailing limbs. "What the fuck!?"

Sadie leapt over the sofa grabbing Todd by the collar, pinning him down to the floor with a knee in his chest. "I am so *fucking* glad I ran into you."

"Who the fuck are you!?" Todd choked out through his shock.

"Sadie Park."

"Little Sadie Park? You work for the mob?" Todd said eyes wide as he stared up at her, struggling to breathe.

"No." Sadie eased off his chest, sure to keep him in place.

"Then what the fuck are you doing here?" Todd asked, putting his hand on her knee, trying to keep it off him.

"Your shithead friends kidnapped Kat," Sadie said.

Todd looked down catching the glint of metal in Sadie's free hand. He stopped his struggling. "Hey! You and Kat are still friends. I always thought you guys would get together." He tilted his head, a coy smile blossoming on his face.

"Did you hear what I said?" Sadie asked, leaning closer to his face.

"They took Kat," Todd said, suddenly serious. "I can guess why. She shouldn't have come back."

"Smartest thing you said so far," Sadie griped. "So, very quickly, tell me what's going on and why you came here."

"Could you let me up off the floor?" Todd asked, resisting the urge to resume his struggling.

"Promise not to run?" Sadie pressed her knee further into his chest.

"I won't run. Considering the heater you got pointed at me."

Sadie looked down at the gun, pulling it aside but not putting it away. She stood, letting Todd up from the ground. "Take a seat."

Todd sat on the couch, readjusting his jacket and dusting himself off. "What happened?"

"That's what I asked," Sadie sighed. Todd watched her, waiting for her response. "Your friends James and Vincent were looking for you and they found Kat. Assholes hit me in the fucking head and took off with her."

"Why is Kat here?" Todd asked.

"Looking for you," Sadie snapped.

"I shouldn't have called her."

"Hey, you said another smart thing," Sadie quipped. Todd scowled at her. "What did you do?"

"It's really hard to explain," Todd said. Sadie squinted at him, mouth set in a grim frown. "Ok. Um. So I owe a lot of money to the mob." Todd's voice cracked. "And I couldn't pay it. So they told me I had to do work. I was running drugs for a while. Everything's going okay. Then one day on a big run I get robbed. It's these guys' rivals. I tell them that. They say I still owe them. They set Jimmy and Vince to 'watch' me. They want us to rob these guys. We get details on the shipment and snag it but Vince and Jim decided on stealing it. But it's my ass on the line so I take it. Now I'm just trying to get the fuck out of dodge."

"Is that why you're here?" Sadie asked.

"They raided my place. Probably for the drugs. Took my passport and my plane ticket outta there. I came looking for 'em."

"They didn't take them," Sadie said. Todd sat up eyeballing her. "I got your plane ticket. But Kat's got your passport."

Todd's brow furrowed at the revelation. "They just want the drugs. And I can give them to 'em but then the mob will kill me."

"And if they kill Kat?" Sadie snapped back.

Todd's jaw stiffened. "They wouldn't."

"Threat's kinda empty if they aren't willing to do violence," Sadie said, staring him down.

Todd swallowed. "What do you want me to do?"

"Come with me to my office and we'll figure out how to get Kat back." Sadie tucked the gun back into her waistband. "And maybe save your life too."

"Well that's a relief," Todd said, standing from the couch. He followed Sadie out the door, shutting it behind them. Outside Sadie watched Todd closely as she hailed a taxi. "We can take the subway."

"No," Sadie said, squinting at him, arm still extended attempting to flag a car down. A yellow taxi pulled up, double parking in the street in front of them. Sadie grabbed Todd by the collar hustling him to the car.

"You don't have to do that." Todd shrugged her off. "I'm going."

Sadie let him go watching expectantly as he climbed in. She followed close behind giving the driver the address for Daedalus. The car pulled off, its occupants immersed in silence.

"Tell me about her?" Todd asked. "Kat."

"Ask her yourself," Sadie answered, investigating him, the ways he'd aged over all these years. How different was he from the man she remembered passing in and out of her best friend's life?

"You're not a very nice daughter-in-law," Todd quipped.

"We're not married," Sadie said.

"That's surprising." Todd had that same easy smile on his face.

That hadn't changed. "She was so in love with you. And she was a *really* gay kid. Wait!" Todd interrupted himself. "Why haven't you popped the question yet?"

"Could you not?" Sadie glared at him before looking out the window. "My head is splitting," she sighed.

"You don't look so great, kid," Todd said, turning sympathetic. Sadie turned back to him, a frown marring her face. "Okay." Todd raised his hands in surrender.

The rest of the ride was quiet as the car navigated the densely packed city. Sadie had been caught off guard when Todd asked about Kat. What did she know about her? She went to Stanford. Kat had told her that years ago when they were in high school, when they were navigating an awkward balance of friendship turned to something more. One of the most confusing times in Sadie's life bar one. She'd picked up on a few things in the short time Kat had been back. Kat and Jaime had broken up. Amicably from the sound of it. Kat lived in L.A., she had a job in PR, she overdosed on something. That gave her pause. There was a whole world of things she didn't know about this woman who felt so familiar. The woman she so desperately wanted to save. What happened in all those lonely years apart?

The cab came to an abrupt halt outside Daedalus Detective Agency. Sadie paid the fare, maintaining a close eye on Todd as he exited the vehicle. The car pulled off leaving just the two of them on the street. Sadie waved him along, climbing the stairs and unlocking the building's front door, ushering Todd in ahead of her. Together they walked up to the office, Sadie keeping behind Todd. Just in case. She unlocked the office letting Todd in before shutting the door behind them, locking it once again.

"Take a seat," Sadie said, depositing herself in her own chair behind the desk. She pulled the file folder out of her waistband and tossed it on the table. Todd sat down leaning forward and taking the folder, opening it and studying its contents.

"Not an attractive photo," he said, looking over Vincent's picture.

"Where do you think they took her?" Sadie asked.

"How should I know," Todd said. "This is your plan."

"You said they want the drugs."

"What else could they want?" Todd asked absently.

"Why don't you just call them and give them the stuff?"

"I don't have their phone number. It's on the burner and I ditched it," Todd said, running a hand through his graying hair.

"Where?"

"With the drugs."

"And they haven't called you?" Sadie asked.

"They don't have my real numbers."

Before Sadie could suggest their next steps a stern knocking came from the front door. They both turned sharply, keenly aware of the intruder. Sadie stood slowly peering at the door. The knocking continued.

"There's a room through there. Shut the door and don't make a sound," Sadie said.

"Okay, boss." Todd got up, disappearing inside the small room.

Sadie approached the door mentally running through a list of who the mystery guest could be. Taking a moment to collect herself, she took a deep breath before easing the door open. On the other side was Daniel's taut face, weary with bags under his eyes, shoulders pinched with stress.

"Thank God you're here," Daniel said the moment he laid eyes on her, searching her face for her condition.

"Did you find anything?" Sadie asked, brow furrowing, standing taller.

"No," Daniel answered, pushing past her into the office. "Just glad you didn't go off and do anything stupid."

Sadie raised her eyebrows letting out a sigh. "What are you doing here? How's the investigation going?"

"I need your written statement," Daniel said, sitting where

Todd had just been. Sadie sat across from him at the desk. "We put out an APB. Nothing yet. I'll be updated when I get back. How's the-" Daniel pointed at his own head indicating Sadie's head wound.

"It's fine," Sadie said. "Give me whatever paper you need me to fill out."

Daniel handed her the form. Sadie grasped it, picking up a pen from her desk and began writing. He watched her patiently, inspecting her exhausted face.

"You should really see a doctor, Sadie." Daniel leaned forward in his seat. "You don't look good."

"You shouldn't say that to a woman," Sadie said, never taking her eyes from the paper.

"You know what I mean."

"Find Kat. Then I'll find a doctor, okay?" Sadie finished writing and passed the form back, pen still in hand. "Please," she said, eyes glossing over with tears. "I need your help."

"We're gonna find her," Daniel said, briefly glancing at the paper. "I know you're not just sitting here idly. I need you to tell me anything you find out. Okay?"

Sadie nodded. "I will."

Daniel stood turning to leave. Halfway to the door, he turned back. "Look, I know you care about this girl, but don't get yourself killed over this. Let us do our job." He turned to leave again, shutting the door behind him with an audible click.

Sadie sat a moment, contemplating her options in the moment of silence. Could she trust the cops? She couldn't trust Todd, but maybe she could steer this situation.

"Who was that?" Todd asked, head poking around a corner.

"A friend," Sadie said, still watching the door. "A cop. He's helping find Kat." Sadie stood walking across the room and locking the door.

"What did you tell him?" Todd came fully around the corner to lean against the wall where he stood.

"That they assaulted and kidnapped Kat 'cause you owe money to the mob." Sadie turned to face him.

"That's it?" Todd pressed.

"Well I didn't know about the drugs then," Sadie said, staring him down.

"You didn't say anything now?"

"I still might." Sadie waved her hand, indicating Todd take a seat. Todd stood in place for a moment, searching the tenseness permeating Sadie's body. He walked back to the desk, sitting once again. "We need to call them. If they haven't called already.

Tell them we'll give them whatever they want."

Todd nodded. "It's all stashed. We just have to go to it."

Sadie stood behind her desk, peering out the window. Outside, on the street below, she watched Daniel's car pull away, finding its way through gaps in traffic before disappearing around a street corner. Sadie picked up her phone calling for a taxi.

"I don't know if using a cab to move this stuff is such a hot idea," Todd said after she hung up.

"They're just taking us. We need to be off the streets as much as possible." Sadie answered, turning from the window to investigate Todd. Despite his facade, there was an underlying anxiety punctuating his 'easy' demeanor. Little things. The stiffening of a jaw, tense shoulders, the small shifts in tone, the way his voice warbled subtly when the cops came up. "What are we moving exactly?"

"Maybe it's better you don't know," Todd said.

"Daniel's extra antsy. He's not saying it, but there's more to this. So I can ask him or you can tell me." Sadie replied, emotionless while she untucked the gun from her waistband and sat it on the desk. Opening a drawer she brought out a box of bullets, placing them next to the pistol. "Cause I think it's very serious"

Todd swallowed, leg bouncing while he eyed Sadie. "It's fentanyl. From China." Todd looked away. "Bad stuff if you ask me, but the people love it."

"So what were you gonna do? Sell the drugs, get people killed, run away with your money?" Sadie asked, jaw clenching as she spoke.

"No different than any guy in the game," Todd answered.

"I should take you to the cops."

"You want Kat back don't you?" Todd cut her off. "They don't give a shit about Kat. Let's just get the stuff, make the trade. I'll disappear forever. Call the cops after."

Sadie stared him down, palms on the desk, leaning against it. "I think our rides here." She took the box and opened it before removing the bullets. Picking up the gun, she opened the cylinder and began loading it. With a decisive click, she closed the cylinder, sliding the bullets into place before tucking the gun away in her waistband. Todd watching her all the while.

"Come on," she said, gesturing for Todd to follow her out of the office.

Together they made it to the street just as the yellow taxi arrived. Sadie opened the car door, waving Todd in. "After you."

"Very gentlemanly of you," Todd said, laughing to himself as he entered the vehicle. "You should really propose to my daughter. So tough. So honorable." He turned to the cabbie, giving him an address for a restaurant, "New Star Diner on 157th street."

Sadie scanned the street before she climbed into the backseat beside Todd, shutting the door firmly behind her. The cab pulled away.

"Happy to know I have your blessing." Sadie rolled her eyes. She peered out the window, ignoring him for now. His comments brought Kat to mind and suddenly she was inundated. Kat's face came to life in her mind. She had never prayed before but now she asked whatever could be listening out there to protect Kat till she could find her. She swore to herself she was going to find her. She wanted to cry, but held back biting her lip and clenching her fists instead. Not in front of Todd. It was bad enough he kept making those jokes, hitting closer to home than he realized. Or maybe he knew exactly what he was doing. At least he wasn't homophobic. That'd make Kat happy.

Across the seat, Todd intermittently watched the young woman beside him between glances out the window, mindful of the route they were taking.

"Is she happy?" Todd asked, breaking the silence.

Sadie turned to him. "I don't know. She seems lost. She seems happy when she's with me."

"Thank you," he said quietly, turning to look out the window. The car pulled up outside a boxcar diner, its neon sign reading 'New Star Diner' flickering on and off, fluorescent stars twinkling next to the font. "This is us."

Sadie paid the driver and pulled Todd out the car. Todd approached the diner's metallic door holding it open for Sadie, waving her into the establishment. The diner was sparsely populated. Several booths were full of customers hunched over their plates talking amicably, their voices blending into the soft music playing. Behind the counter stood an elderly woman with dyed black hair, the roots growing out, showing traces of gray. The woman spotted them immediately.

"Where you been, asshole!?" she shouted across the diner.

"I like her," Sadie said to Todd, smiling despite herself.

"Hey, Mira!" Todd approached the bar and placed both hands on the countertop, lifting himself half over it to give Mira a kiss on the cheek. She smiled big and slapped him playfully on the shoulder, "I just need to grab my stuff from the back."

"Oh, okay!" She nodded, still smiling. "It's right where you left it. Do you have time to eat? You and your friend."

"Not today, Mira. I'm sorry," Todd said, face full of sincerity.

"That's okay. I'll make you a couple to go boxes. What do you want?"

"The usual," Todd answered. "Sadie?" He turned to her.

"A burger. Please." Sadie answered, distractedly looking around the diner, taking in all the faces around them.

Todd waved for Sadie to follow him across the restaurant and through a kitchen door. In the kitchen were two cooks talking nonchalantly till Mira put in the order. One of the cooks grabbed the receipt and began working on their meals, easy laughter passing between the pair. Todd went down a narrow hallway opening a door to a small office overflowing with cabinets and papers. Tucked in the corner was a small foot locker. He pulled a key from his pocket, unlocked a padlock, and opened the lid revealing two large black duffle bags in pristine condition. He reached in, lifting one and passing it to Sadie. She took it, slinging the bag's strap across her body. Unzipping it she saw tightly wrapped bricks of powder.

"How much is this worth?" she asked, zipping it shut again.

"More than both of us," Todd sighed, pulling a clunky cell phone from the other bag before slinging the strap on one shoulder. He began pressing buttons on the device till the room filled with a man's tinny voice emanating from the cheap plastic.

"Look, Todd, we got your kid." In the background a muffled scuffle, voices muted. One sounded like Kat arguing. "If you know what's good for you, you'll meet us and make a trade."

The line disconnected.

Todd called the number back, taking the phone off speaker. He pressed the cell to his ear listening intently to the dial tone. For long moments there was no answer. Sadie watched him anxiously.

"Hey, Vin," Todd said, voice even and serious. "Got your message." Todd fell quiet, listening closely, every now and again mumbling an affirmative. "Okay. Tonight." Todd hung up. "They want to make the trade tonight at 2 AM. They're going to call with a location right before."

"Then we'll be prepared," Sadie said, shifting the bag against herself. They left the office together, Todd shutting the door behind himself. The cooks had fallen into idle chatter again, ignoring them as they left.

Out in the dining room, Mira was there with two to-go containers waiting on the counter for them. Todd grabbed one, opening the lid before passing it to Sadie and taking the other one.

"Thanks, Mira," he said, pulling out his wallet from his back pocket. Mira waved it away.

"On me," she said, reaching out and pinching his cheek.

"I won't be back for a long time," Todd replied.

"Be safe, okay?" Mira said with an affectionate smile.

"I'll try." Todd laughed, kissing her on the cheek before turning to leave.

"Thank you," Sadie said to Mira before following close behind. The woman waved after them before returning to her duties. "We should move fast, get to my office, and lay low till it's time."

She opened her container, eating french fries as they walked quickly to Daedalus. Todd pulled a sandwich from his, disposing of the box in a nearby trash bin, balancing it on top of a mound of overflowing garbage. They walked in silence, delicately maneuvering around pedestrians, keeping as discreet as possible. Sadie trailed closely at Todd's side, keeping an eye on him while keeping aware of the humming world around them.

Sadie felt a brief wave of relief when they turned off the busy, overcrowded main street into a rare quiet one. Scarcely any people lingered, it was mostly empty save the rows of parked cars lining the streets. Sadie moved to cross in the middle of the road eager to shorten their journey when the roar of an engine tore through the street, echoing off the brick and cement buildings, amplifying the noise. Sadie turned to the sound only to catch the sunlight bouncing off the metallic chrome of a fender before the sudden earth-shattering collision like a wall falling on top of her. A crash of riotous pain shot through her body, seering through nerve endings as she folded. Rolling atop the hood of the car she careened with the glass filling her ears with a sound like thick ice cracking in spiderwebs all at once. She flew off the bumper, through the air till she collided with pavement, rolling in a skid across the cement, bag still fixed to her, alternately hitting her and padding the fall.

When Sadie came to a stop she gasped in a shuddering breath, fighting to breathe against the shock of pain tearing through her body. A sharp ringing punctuated her eardrums and the smell of oil and gas and exhaust flooded her nostrils. The side of her face throbbed, wetness dripping down her cheek to her chin. The car stood still several yards away, engine still rumbling. A man got out of the driver's side and approached her, hovering over her while she writhed on the ground.

"That's what you get for spying on me," he said, grasping her face so she'd look at him. "My wife left me 'cause of you!"

"You're a fucking psychopath, Nate," Sadie answered through the haze of pain.

"Hey! That's my kid's girl!" Todd screamed, colliding into Nate, simultaneously hitting him in the head with the heavy duffle bag, sending them both tumbling to the ground in a twisted heap of limbs. Todd started swinging wildly while Nate struggled furiously to detangle himself.

Sadie groaned, forcing herself to her hands and knees, slowly standing despite the stabbing pain. She dropped the duffel bag before pulling Todd off the other man. Grasping Nate by the collar, she punched him solidly in the face.

"Did you hurt Anna?" Sadie asked fist poised to punch Nate again.

"What?" he asked dumbfounded. Sadie punched him again, her knuckles forcibly colliding with his nose till blood poured from it.

"You hit me with a car! Did you hurt Anna?" Sadie asked again.

"No!" Nate said, clutching his nose.

Sadie glanced around, seeing no one she drew her gun from her waistband, pressing it into his chin till the barrel left a divot in his skin, she spoke quietly, "I'm going to check on her. And if she's not okay I'm going to come for you. You got me?"

"Yeah." Nate nodded against the gun.

Sadie pulled the gun away, tucking it back into her waistband. Lifting Nate up by his shirt till he stood unsteadily on his own two feet. She shoved him forcefully in the direction of the car. Todd watched on wide-eyed. "We need to get off the streets." She picked the bag off the ground, slinging it over her shoulder, face grimacing in obvious pain as she clutched her side.

"Let me take that," Todd said, hand outstretched for the bag.

"Now you want to be a gentleman," Sadie grumbled, thrusting the bag in his direction. She grabbed Nate again, pushing him into the driver's seat through the open door. "You're gonna drive us somewhere and you're not gonna do anything stupid," she said. Todd climbed into the backseat while Sadie rounded the car getting into the passenger seat. She drew the gun again keeping it low. "I bet you already know where my office is." Nate nodded solemnly, glancing down at the gun. "Drive."

"Uh," Todd said from the back. "I hate to interrupt all...this, but Sadie you should go to the fucking hospital."

Sadie chuckled. "And let you get away. Never."

"I'm-I'm not gonna run away. Can we just go before you

fucking drop dead?"

"Only if Daniel keeps an eye on you," Sadie said, groaning as she clutched her side, gun still trained on Nate as he drove.

Todd's eyes shifted nervously, assessing the situation. His face was beaded with sweat. He ran the back of his hand against his forehead, wiping it away. "Fine."

"Here," Sadie said, thrusting her phone in Todd's direction. "Call him."

"Can't you?" Todd shrugged, eyebrow raised in distaste.

"I'm a little fucking busy, Todd." Sadie tilted the gun in emphasis.

"Fuck. Fine!" Todd pulled up Detective Daniel Guinto on the phone and with a sigh pressed the call button. The phone rang and rang. Todd swallowed suddenly feeling sick. The line answered.

"Hello, Sadie-" Daniel started.

"Nah. It's Todd. Todd Everett. I heard you wanted to talk to me. Can you meet me at..." Todd pulled the phone from his face. "What's the closest hospital?"

"Bloomfield General," Nate answered, squinting to see through the cracks in the windshield.

"Bloomfield General," Todd repeated into the phone. "Like ASAP. Before I lose my fucking nerve." He hung up the phone, passing it back to Sadie.

"You won't tell them?" Nate asked. "What I did to you?"

Sadie gritted her teeth. "Is that what you're worried about right now?"

Nate drove faster till they came barrelling up to the hospital's doors. He pulled into the drive right to the entrance where Todd came spilling out the back, both duffel bags strapped to him. He flung the passenger door open and helped Sadie from the car, being careful of her obvious wounds.

"Hey!" Todd yelled into the hospital's open doors. "A little fucking help!"

Blue and red lights came pouring into the parking lot making the hospital walls glow. Nate went peeling off out of the lot and as far away as he could get.

Sadie blinked rapidly, feeling the world rush in and out of existence. Everything was spinning and it made her sick to her stomach. "Todd," she groaned, using the last of her strength. "You better not run away. We gotta save Kat."

"Don't worry. I'm right here, kid."

Everything faded into a soft nothingness as doctors came rushing out the doors with a stretcher.

"I'm trusting you."

Chapter Four

Kat listened intently through the crack in the door. Hushed voices drifted through. She strained to catch their meaning. The men had blindfolded her after dragging her half-naked from Sadie's apartment and throwing her into the back of a car. She had struggled against them till the ugly guy with the flattened nose grabbed her by the throat, pulling a gun and telling her to stop. One word. Stop. Then the blindfold and a zip tie around her wrists for good measure. Everything in her screamed to panic. She swallowed the instinct down, packing it into a box, nice and neat for later. Instead, she forced herself to listen. The same man told her if she made a scene she'd go in the trunk. Kat jerked forward with the car's sudden movement. Neither man spoke during the drive. There was nothing telling about the outside world besides the sounds of train cars, the clack of rails, and the ringing bells. Soon she was pulled from the car and marched into somewhere. A hand shoved her into this room before removing the blindfold. A darkened bedroom. The bald man flipped a switch filling the room with a dim grungy light. He pulled a knife out approaching her, keeping the sharpened blade between them.

"Will you be good?" he asked.

Kat nodded hesitantly. The bald man grabbed her by the wrists holding her still and with a quick jerk he sliced the restraints off. Kat instantly rubbed her wrists where the plastic had bit into the skin. The man put the knife away. Taking a bottle of water from a nearby card table he handed it to her. She took it delicately, careful not to touch him.

"Let's hope this doesn't take long," he said before leaving her alone, keeping the door slightly ajar so they could keep one eye on her from the living room.

That had been hours ago.

From what she could tell Jimmy was the one with the busted nose and Vince was the bald one. Vince seemed a little sharper than Jimmy who seemed more violent. Quite the duo. Kat listened to their quiet conversation, filtering it against the sounds of a television playing softly in the living room. She searched the room contemplating a means of escape. On the far wall was a window. Its glass panes were blacked out with paint leaving only clumpy splotches where light could spill through. It was morning now. Nails came protruding from the wood of the window frame, sealing it shut. They were prepared. Or they'd done this before. Kat sat on the bed, straining to hear. Jimmy and Vince seemed increasingly agitated.

"I can't believe Todd fucked us like this!" Jimmy said, chugging a beer as he paced the living room floor. "What are we gonna do?"

"We're doing it." Vince sat on the sofa intently watching the television. A news report droned on, murmuring about a recent explosion. The anchor's monologue only frustrated Jimmy more. He finished the beer, crushing the empty can and tossing it across the room where it collided with the wall. Vince didn't react. "Todd will trade the drugs for the girl and we'll get the fuck out of here."

"Yeah before one of these fucking assholes finds us?" Jimmy asked, cracking open another beer. "We got the mob waiting on us, those drug dealer pricks after us, and now the cops. We should never have let Todd talk us into keeping that shit! Shoulda known he'd fuck us over!"

"Would you calm the fuck down?" Vince said, eyes trained on Jimmy, leaning forward in his seat, elbows balanced on his knees.

"What are we gonna do?" Jimmy said, his voice half slurred with alcohol.

"What do you want to do?" Vince snapped.

"Tell the mob Todd ripped us off. Let them sort it out," Jimmy answered.

"And when they talk to Todd?"

"They'd believe us."

"Or they'd get rid of all of us. Wash their hands clean of this fucking mess." Vince sighed.

"So what do we do?" Jimmy asked.

"We wait." Vince muted the television. "Lay low till we find Todd. When we get the drugs we can decide what comes next."

Inside the bedroom Kat laid back, brow furrowed as her mind frantically raced. Of course her dad had gotten himself into the shittiest mess possible. In the lonely quiet room that smelled of must and mold, she felt all the things she'd tucked away unravel and spill forth. She was going to get killed because of her father and all she could think was to run to Sadie. She desperately wanted to know if she was okay. Desperately wanted to apologize for so much before these men killed her when Todd inevitably disappointed them. Silent tears fell from the corners of her eyes. She shut them tight, cutting herself off from this place. She imagined she was with Sadie, entwined together. Her heart ached at the thought. Opening her eyes she began puzzling together a plan, something she could do to escape this.

"I'm going out," Jimmy grunted, already halfway out the door.

"Jim, come on! You know that's a shit idea," Vince called after him, quickly standing, staying close at his heels. It didn't matter though.

"Whatever." Jimmy slammed the front door in Vince's face making the cheap plaster walls rattle.

Vince wound his arm back, fist clenched and ready to punch the wall. Before he could strike out, he stopped, breathing deeply before lowering his fist. Going to the window he peeked out the blinds seeing Jimmy climb into the beat-up car and peel out, leaving a cloud of smoke and dust in his wake.

"He sounds upset," Kat said sardonically, watching on from the doorway.

"Shut it," Vince answered, still looking out the blinds.

"Why do you put up with him? Isn't he gonna fuck up whatever stupid plans you have?" Kat prodded, anxiety already pooling in her gut, but unable to stop herself.

"You know how family is," Vince said, looking over his shoulder at her.

"Jimmy's what? Your brother?" Kat asked.

Vince turned to face her, eyes scrutinizing her. "I guess so."

"Why are you doing all this?" Kat asked, stepping out of the room. Vince didn't say anything, instead, he picked up a gun off the table and slipped it into the waistband of his pants. "Okay..." Kat paused. "Wanna know why I'm here?"

"Not really," Vince said, sitting on the sofa and grabbing a beer, eyes scarcely leaving Kat.

"Todd called me. Said he owed $80 grand to someone. I bet you owe something to them too." Vince's eyebrows furrowed, he continued watching her, staying silent. "Fucked up stuff

121

happens when you owe money, huh? Especially when family's involved."

"No kidding," Vince said, cracking his beer open and taking a swig. He took an unopened one and tossed it to Kat. She caught it deftly.

"We lost everything. Over and over again 'cause of him," Kat said, investigating the beer's label.

"Guess we're not that different, you and me," Vince said.

"How's that?"

"We both got fucked over by your dad," Vince finished the beer and stood up, going to the window to look out. "It's the mob. He owed to the mob. My dad did too. He started working for them, then we did too. I never wanted any of this shit. I just wanted to get out." Vince turned again to look at Kat. "Get back in the room." He pulled the gun out of his waistband and waved it casually at Kat. "I'm done with our little Q and A."

Kat nodded, setting the beer down and retreating, leaving Vince alone with his frantic thoughts.

Across town Jimmy arrived at the bar, already feeling calmer but still desperately in need of a few hard drinks. He was suffocating in that shit hole with his brother and Todd's kid, their apparent hostage. Not that he ever agreed to all that. He sat at the bar, across from the bartender.

"Hey, Andrea right? Get me a few shots of whiskey?" Jimmy pulled his wallet out, producing some bills and setting them on the countertop.

"Sure thing," Andy said, turning to glance at the bottles on the wall. "You look like you're having a hard night. Why don't I get you the good stuff, on the house?"

Jimmy smiled and tucked the money back in his pocket. Andy crossed the bar and grabbed a pricey bottle off a high shelf. Setting it down she discreetly slipped her phone out of her pocket and wrote out a text.

'Your guy is at the bar. The ugly one. Hurry!'

Far away, in a hospital bed, Sadie slowly came to. The sterile scent of bleach filled her nostrils. The low mumble of a building full of people going about hectic lives flooded her senses. She had dreamt again in her pained haze, everything extra vivid in the foggy mist of the drugs the doctors had pumped her full of. Her mind conjured up visions of Kat. Safe and in her arms, both of them far from this place. Kat. So close she could kiss her. So close she could breathe in her smell, feel the heat of her body pressed into her. The dream had felt so safe that waking in this hospital bed seemed a cruel joke.

"You're awake," Daniel said from the doorway.

"Is that what this awful pain is?" Sadie asked, forcing herself up into a sitting position, wincing all the while.

"Well, you sound like yourself, so you probably don't have brain damage." Daniel entered the room pulling a chair up to the bedside and sitting. His face was weary, large bags encircling his eyes, clothes wrinkled and dirty.

"Where's Todd?" Sadie ignored his question, carefully investigating her bandages while she waited for an answer.

"At the police station giving his statement," Daniel answered, trying to catch her attention. "Did Dumb and Dumber do this to you?"

"No," Sadie said, looking him in his dark eyes. "What's going on?"

"Doctor says you have a couple fractured ribs and a mild concussion, but no worse for wear."

Sadie gave him a blank look. "Okay."

"You really don't-" Daniel began before cutting himself off. "Todd's made a deal with the police. A full confession and helping us put away a lot of bad people. Including James and Vincent."

"So he's confessing to stealing the drugs?"

"The explosion. At the docks," Daniel answered. "Handing over that fentanyl bought him a lot of favor with the Chief."

Sadie's brow pinched, her mouth fell open in shock. "He didn't tell me about the explosion."

"I wonder why." Daniel rolled his eyes.

"What does Todd get?"

"Aside from getting Kat back? He'll get off scot-free. They'll hold him till a trial then witness protection most likely."

"We need to get Kat," Sadie said, already pulling the hospital machine's wires off herself.

"We are," Daniel said, standing and grasping her hands to stop her. "The trade is tonight. The arrangements are made. You don't need to do anything but wait."

Sadie scoffed, shrugging Daniel off. "I don't have to stay here. You said it yourself, I'm fine."

"I didn't say that," Daniel sighed. "Look, I need to go and you need to stay here."

"Okay," Sadie said, face curiously blank.

"Sadie," Daniel said, exasperation settling into his voice as his patience slipped. "You need to stay for observation and you *need* to not interfere. Don't make me station an officer at your door."

"Fine," Sadie huffed, looking like a petulant child stuck in the sterile bed.

"Promise."

"Fine. I promise," Sadie groaned. "Go get Kat. Please." Pain flickered across her face, turning her mouth into a grimace.

"I promise." Daniel nodded, concern pinching his features. His phone rang cutting through the room. With a final glance, he disappeared out the hospital doors leaving Sadie alone with her pain. Alone with all the thoughts she'd been holding at bay. She needed to see Kat. Was frightened for her as she imagined the millions of possible scenarios she might be experiencing. The cops were going to get Kat killed in their excitement for a 'win' against the mob. She needed to get out of here.

To her left was a small side table. Someone had placed her personal effects on top including her phone and clothes. Of course her gun was nowhere to be seen. Unarmed then. Pressing a button on her phone the screen lit up displaying the time and a text message from Andy. One of the guys was at the bar with Andy. The message was from hours ago.

Sadie hit the call button praying that Andy would answer. It only took two rings before Andy's familiar voice was there.

"Where are you?" Andy said, straight to the point.

"Its been hectic, to say the least," Sadie answered. "Are you okay? What happened with the guy?"

"Jimmy was here when I texted you. For a drink. He said his name was Jimmy. He seemed upset. Went on about his family getting him into some fucked up shit. He was here maybe an hour. I stalled as long as I could."

"Did he say where he was going?" Sadie asked, forcing herself to sit up, biting back the sting of pain so Andy wouldn't hear.

"No. He mentioned leaving town soon, but that's it."

"Andy, if you see Jimmy again, call the cops, okay? Right away."

"Sadie, what's going on? Are you alright?" panic slipped into Andy's voice, something she always fought to hide from her.

"I can't talk right now. But let's meet up. After this case, in a day or two." Sadie answered, avoiding Andy's real questions.

"Sadie-" Andy started, but Sadie was already hanging up.

It was still hours before the exchange. And she had no idea where the trade off would be. Another problem to add to the ever growing list of problems. Reining herself in Sadie began with the first step. Getting out of the hospital. The doctors and nurses seemed preoccupied with another busy night. Sadie delicately slipped the hospital devices off, keeping alert for anything that might draw unwanted attention. She stood up carefully unsure how this would go. Her whole body ached and pain throbbed throughout despite the painkillers they'd given her. Gritting her teeth she reached for her clothes taking the jeans that were neatly folded from the bottom. These weren't the clothes she came in with. Daniel's doing? At least her jacket had somehow remained intact. Bending over hurt worse. Sadie bit her lip forcing the pants around her legs, struggling to pull them up against the radiating pain of her fractured ribs.

"I should not be doing this," she sighed under her breath, buttoning the jeans. Taking a moment to steady herself, she looked around making sure no one was near. Grabbing the rest of her possessions she shuffled to the nearby bathroom. Closing the toilet seat she set everything down before turning back to close the door, locking it once it clicked shut. Her hand traced the wall till her fingertips met cold plastic. With a firm press of the button the light came on filling the tiny stall in a sickly fluorescent glow. Forcing herself away from the door Sadie turned, coming face to face with her reflection. She looked washed out in the crinkled hospital gown. Her face was partially swollen around her hairline, her lip was split open, an angry red line cut across it. Around her cheekbone a light purpling had begun to emerge. With a deep breath, Sadie pulled the gown off, lifting its loose collar over her head, freeing herself from it and tossing it aside, letting it fall discarded to the floor. In the mirror she made out a world of bruises, a myriad of colors, sprawling out like a galaxy just beneath her skin. The bruising was worse around her ribs, where she had taken the brunt of the car full force. Her shoulder was a close contender, a large bruise spiraled out from the socket to her arm and up to her collarbone. She'd never been hit by a car before. It definitely ranked on worst experiences. Sadie reached for her bra, holding it with both hands before examining her ribcage. Foregoing the garment, she reached for her t-shirt instead, grateful it was loose. With a pained gasp, she pulled the shirt over her head. She grasped onto the sink feeling a sudden rush of dizziness. The world fell out of focus as she forced herself to breathe through it. That's pretty bad, but at least she was dressed. She reached for her jacket, easing her arms into the sleeves, feeling a little more prepared and grateful she wasn't dizzy. There was still the matter of shoes. Turning the faucet on she splashed water on her face letting it soothe her heated skin. Not bothering to dry off she eased herself onto the toilet seat reaching for one shoe, fighting her body's screams of protest. Her nerve endings felt frayed from the searing shockwaves of pain. Slowly and deliberately she put her shoes on.

With the task done Sadie forced herself up using the sink for leverage. Sighing deeply she opened the bathroom door walking out as though nothing was amiss. The bedside table held her wallet, keys, and phone. She picked them up, slipping the items into her jacket's pockets. The hallway outside was quiet, mostly desolate aside from a few milling doctors and nurses, too exhausted and busy to notice one out of place patient. Casually strolling out the door she forced herself to ignore the pain radiating from her ribs and to keep a straight face. At the end of the hallway was an elevator, the car just arrived, its doors sliding open letting a few people in plain clothes out. Sadie slipped past them hurriedly pressing the ground floor button. The door closed leaving her in an empty elevator. She leaned against the elevator wall, face away from the camera prominently displayed in the corner. Luckily the elevator didn't stop on its descent and she was safely deposited on the ground floor where the world's pace was much faster. Outside the elevator doors everything was a flurry of movement. People rushed around in a swirl of chaotic noise. By the nurse's station were two uniformed cops casually leaning against the nurse's desk, not doing anything in particular but sipping on their coffee.

On a nearby wall was a placard, arrows pointed in different directions leading the way. In the opposite direction was a dingy white arrow indicating a gift shop. Sadie raised an eyebrow but followed the direction turning her back to the cops. A few solitary people roamed the shop's cramped aisles, a bored looking middle-aged woman manned the register in front. Sadie kept her head down avoiding eye contact. A nearby rack held rows of sweatshirts in every color. Sadie picked one in black and found a shelf of aspirin and other bottles. She grabbed a couple of bottles haphazardly before fishing for a water bottle from a nearby refrigerator.

"Did you hear what they're saying on the news?" a man asked a woman he was with, as they strolled the cramped shop's aisles, unaware of the quiet they interrupted. "The explosion?" The woman shook her head no. "They're starting to report how many people died. It's crazy. The cops won't say it's terrorists."

Sadie forced herself to look away from the couple. She went to the counter putting the items down, wallet already half out. The woman scarcely looked at her as she rung up the items, her attention instead transfixed on a muted television mounted to the far wall. She collected Sadie's cash, passing her a receipt distractedly.

"Thanks," Sadie said, taking the newly bagged items and slipping into a nearby bathroom. Finding a stall she took her jacket off, letting out a small gasp of pain before pulling the sweatshirt on. She pulled its hood over her head, tucking her hair back till it disappeared. Feeling satisfied Sadie put her jacket back on before putting the bottle of aspirin in her jacket pocket.

Back in the hallway, she walked past the nurse's station where the cops still lingered. Neither bothered looking her way as they laughed among themselves. Sadie marched through the hospital doors amid the chaos of everyday life as it rushed all around her. Nearby was a row of taxis idling while they waited for potential fares as they came out the doors. Sadie hailed the closest one.

"Where to?" the driver asked as she climbed inside, shutting the door firmly behind her.

"The police station. On Fairfax and Lennox."

The driver nodded, pulling the car away from the curb and out of the small lot. "Looks like it's been a rough one," he said with a weary smile and a quick glance at her in the rearview.

"What's your name?" Sadie asked, looking at the back of his head as he drove.

"Eddie," he answered over his shoulder.

"It's been fucking horrible, Eddie," Sadie sighed.

"Want to talk about it?" he asked, weaving through city traffic.

"Not really. Just...just get us there quick. It's important."

"You got it, boss," he said, somehow pushing the car faster as they dodged the litany of cars in their way. In no time they came turning onto the street where the police station was.

"Slow down," Sadie said from the backseat. "Let me out here." Eddie pulled the car over into a miraculously empty space. "What do I owe you?"

"Don't worry about it," Eddie said, instead producing a business card. "Here. Call me if you need a ride." Sadie took the card tucking it into her pocket.

"Thanks," she said before smiling at him, he smiled back, face warm and open. "Actually. Can you wait here for me? I won't be long."

"Yeah." Eddie nodded. "I won't move."

"Thanks." She jogged off, opting to take an alleyway she knew led to a back door at the station. The alleyway seemed oppressively dark and stunk of damp garbage. The door was on the far edge, close to the dumpsters and a small loading dock. A small band of light spilled from the ajar door. Sadie approached, curious to find it already open, just a crack. She pulled it further open, slipping inside and closing the door behind her. The back hall was empty. Pulling her hood tighter she rushed through the corridor, listening intently for signs of life. At the other end of the hall was a metal door. Sadie approached cautiously, pushing it open just enough to see beyond. The other side was full of life as cops buzzed around handling their nightly routines. A few cops were on the far side of the first room talking among themselves while they eyeballed three men handcuffed to chairs. The bullpen was a tangle of people, coming and going, distracted. Too distracted to notice anything amiss. To the left was a stairway leading up to rooms where they questioned suspects and held people. Sadie closed the door gently. Todd was probably being held upstairs. She didn't need him though. She just needed to know where the exchange was happening. There was probably intel on Daniel's desk. Or wherever they planned their operations. Odds were Daniel was too busy to be sitting around at his desk.

Opening the door again she walked out, hood still on. She strode confidently while still clinging to a wall, keeping a low profile. Most times acting like you were exactly where you belonged kept questions away. Daniel's desk was towards the far corner of the bullpen. She couldn't see him from her vantage. She made a line for his desk, avoiding walking through the maze of office space. Towards the center of the bullpen, two detectives were exchanging workplace gossip. Sadie slowed, spotting a water fountain next to her. She turned, leaning over it and taking a long drink.

"You think it'll go smooth?" the younger detective asked.

"Who knows," the older one answered, voice weary and grizzled. "They'll do what they can."

"And the girl?"

"The mayor's more anxious to prove that explosion wasn't terrorists. Busting these guys puts a lot of minds at ease and makes us look like heroes. And we need that bad."

"Our image isn't too good after-"

"I know," the older one cut in.

Sadie's brow furrowed. She'd stopped drinking water, instead, she fought the sudden spike in anger. They really didn't care what happened to Kat. She turned back to the task at hand, walking towards Daniel's desk with purpose. Along the opposite wall, a guy in a baseball cap and sunglasses maneuvered quickly, not bothering with pretense as he reached the bottom of the staircase. He jogged briskly up the steps disappearing out of sight. Sadie stopped in her tracks watching him despite the busy rush of the station. Hairs stood on end on the back of her neck. Something was wrong. She followed close after, staying as obscured as possible. Passing Daniel's desk, Sadie stopped only a moment, staring it down before forcing herself to walk past and climb the stairs, keeping her pace even and unhurried.

Upstairs was empty. Uncomfortably so. Just a wide empty hallway with rows of closed doors leading to who knows what. Far away the faint sound of typing rang against the tile floors. Walking down the hall she peered at each door hoping for something. Midway down was a large glass window, on the other side rows of white chairs and tables facing a whiteboard. Bits of printer paper and maps were taped along it. One map was in the center of the board. Circled and marked with an x, more x's surrounding it. Squinting Sadie made out the train track route leading to the city's northern rail yard. Next to the map were black and white photos, softly grainy like they were enlarged. Of Vince and Jimmy, both men holding placards and facing the camera for their mugshots. The exchange point. The north rail yard. But where did the guy go?

Sadie inched down the hall listening intently. On the right was a door, its placard prominently displayed 'Interrogation Room 1'. Looking around, the hall was still empty. Sadie pressed her ear close to the door, hoping to catch some indication of the other side. A soft thump and sounds of struggle emanated through the dense wood. Turning the handle she found the door somehow unlocked. Giving it a shove, the door scarcely budged. She pushed harder till the door gave, just enough for her to see inside. The body of an unconscious officer was propped against the door, half slumped over and sprawled on the floor. Against the opposite wall was Todd struggling in the man in the hat's grip. The guy had both hands pressed into Todd's throat, crushing into his windpipe. Todd's face was a bright, purpling red. Sadie shoved her way further into the room, grabbing a discarded chair knocked to the ground, and with a huge swing brought it down on the man's head, sending him toppling over. Pain lanced through her abdomen and she came tumbling to the floor, biting back a scream. Todd gasped in choking breaths as he slid to the floor. The man started moving against the chair on top of him. Sadie gasped, forcing herself back to her feet and sprung on top of him, the metal chair still half stuck between them. She brought her fist down over and over into his temple till the man collapsed, falling limp and unconscious.

"Holy shit!" Todd's voice was raspy, straining as he stuttered his words out.

"Who is he?" Sadie asked breathing deeply against the pain radiating throughout her, threatening to knock her unconscious too.

"How the fuck should I know?" Todd answered. "One of the millions uh people that want me dead. You okay, kid?"

"No," Sadie said, shaking her head and forcing herself to stand. "I'm going to get Kat." Bending over the unconscious man, she searched him, taking a gun from the man's waistband. "Wait five minutes then scream for help," Sadie instructed a still gasping Todd. "Tell them what happened. Leave me out of it."

Todd nodded. "The exchange is at the train yard. I'm supposed to meet Vince and Jimmy alone with the stuff in an hour."

Sadie listened, poking her head out the door, searching for signs of life. She turned back to Todd brow furrowed, tucking the gun into her pants. "You should have told me about the explosion. People died."

"I know," Todd answered, struggling to stand. "Go save my kid. Keep her safe."

Sadie only nodded before slipping back out the door. Every step sent sharp stings of pain through her. She jostled down the steps casually biting the inside of her cheek to keep the signs of pain away. No one paid her any mind. She slipped back out the door she came from and back into the alley. Giving up any pretense, Sadie let the pain twist her features into an anguished expression. She moved as quickly as she could getting back onto the street. Spotting Eddie still parked where he said he'd be, she smiled with relief. Behind her police officers began scrambling back into the building. She approached the car as casually as possible while everyone else on the street stared at the flurry of cops.

Back inside Eddie's car Sadie settled into the seat, biting her lip to stifle sounds of pain. She grabbed the water from the seat beside her, pulled the aspirin bottle from her jacket pocket, hastily swallowing a few of the capsules.

"Can you get me near the train yard on the north side?" Sadie asked. Eddie turned to watch her from the driver's seat.

"Yeah," he answered. "Is all that about you?"

"Not really," she replied, breathing deeply. "We should get outta here."

Eddie nodded, eyes half dazed. He turned back around, starting the engine and pulling away from the curb and into traffic. Driving past the police entrance Sadie caught glimpses of the police suddenly hurried and panicked.

One more hour.

A short three miles from the train yard Kat sat idly in the bedroom. The men had given up talking hours ago. Instead, they moved around preparing for the trade off. By some stroke of luck, her dad had called to negotiate the exchange. Vince had placed the phone on speaker after silencing Jimmy. And then, distantly, through the broken seams of a door, she heard her father's voice again. He was tired, oddly sterile, but what did she know, she hadn't seen him in more than a decade. Still, it was different than his last phone call. He let Vince control the conversation, scarcely talking except to agree and confirm. In less than a minute it was set. Somehow Kat didn't feel better. But maybe she'd be back with Sadie soon. That filled her with a sense of relief. For a moment she allowed her thoughts to pull her away from this room, taking her away. To somewhere with Sadie. Somewhere safe. Where Sadie was close enough to reach, to touch and whisper that things would be okay.

The door creaked open, breaking Kat from her momentary escape. Vince's frame filled the doorway. Kat took a step back, away from him. He eyed her quietly.

"What's happening?" Kat asked.

"We're leaving soon," Vince answered, pulling a pair of handcuffs out and showing them to Kat. She stayed still, unsure of what to do. He approached gesturing with a pointed finger for her wrists. With a glare, Kat reluctantly presented her hands. Vince opened the cuffs, wrapping the cold metal around her wrists, and slipping them shut with a simple click. Kat swallowed, feeling an icy pit in her stomach. She clenched her jaw, forcing herself to breathe against her panic. "C'mon."

Vince nudged her out the bedroom door, leading her through

a darkened hallway that smelt of mildew, his hand at the small of her back all the while. At the end of the hall was a wooden door, its paint grimy and peeling off in long curls. Vince reached beyond her, shoving the door open. He didn't bother blindfolding her before pushing her forward. Outside the night air was frigid against her skin, and her breath misted in pale clouds that drifted away. At the bottom of a set of concrete stairs was a parked car. Jimmy leaned against the trunk, smoking a cigarette, its tip glowing red in the night. Seeing them he stubbed the cigarette out on the bumper and flicked it away before spitting. He rounded the car, opening the rear door. In the distance, the sound of trains clacking, its horn cutting through the night.

Sadie heard the trains call from the backseat of Eddie's taxi, stopped half a mile away from the train yard. The pain had subsided some. Enough so she could think a little clearer. The clock was ticking down and so far Sadie couldn't make any of the places the cops could have hidden away. The darkened road was devoid of people. Every few yards a streetlamp created pools of light. They were parked in a darkened spot, tucked in an alley between abandoned warehouses and dilapidated, boarded up homes.

"How well do you know this area?" Sadie asked Eddie, his face silhouetted in the shadows of the cab's interior.

"I know everywhere," he replied, turning in his seat to look at her.

"I saw a map," Sadie said, pausing to picture the map in her head. "I need to get where the decommissioned train cars are kept."

Eddie thought for a moment. "They keep those near the west yard, near the shipping containers." He pointed out the windshield, towards the right. "Go that way, turn down Foster. You'll see it through the fence."

"Thank you, Eddie," Sadie said, looking him in the eye. "Here." She dug a bill out from her coat.

"Nah." Eddie waved it off. "I don't know what kinda fucked up night you're having, but I'm happy to help."

"Thanks." Sadie smiled before sliding out the back. She pulled the hood of her sweatshirt over her head as she walked away from the taxi navigating the alley behind the row homes running parallel to the street. Eddie's car didn't move as Sadie rounded a corner out of sight. She clung to the shadows, moving slowly, alert to anything that could happen. The world was desolate aside from a stray cat. The cat watched her from its perch atop a fence, its eyes following her before delicately leaping to the ground. The little cat ran after her, following closely in her wake. Turning the corner, keeping close to the building's edge Sadie peered across the street, scanning the road, catching glimpses of what she could of the train yard. Everything was eerily peaceful. In the distance was the signpost for Foster street. Fencing began not far from the street corner's lamp post. Giving the road another scan Sadie ran across the street, staying in the dark till she got to Foster. She followed the fence, her furry companion still chasing close behind. The top of the fence was rimmed with barbed wire, preventing anyone from climbing over. All of it looked rusted and worn. The little cat ran past Sadie, rushing ahead. A rat ran adjacent to them, scurrying towards the gutter. The cat leapt at it, missing the rat, causing it to panic and run through the fence. The cat ran close after climbing through a jagged tear in the fencing after its prey. Sadie followed after, pulling on the tear till it opened just enough for her to slip inside.

On the other side, she found the closest cover in the shadows of an enormous metal shipping container. The yard was silent. No dogs or guards. Only the distant echo of trains moving in the night.

Where was everybody?

Chapter Five

The police station was swarmed with officers, all of them overcome with a sudden sense of chaos. Confusion had settled in once Todd had screamed for help from the interrogation room where the Captain had shoved him till the operation began, only bothering to post a solitary officer to stand guard. When the scream came Daniel had been cautiously pacing outside the Captain's office. His secretary had said he was deep in a meeting with the Police Chief and Mayor. The moment Todd's voice tore through the station Daniel had abandoned his post running towards the cry for help. The door to the office opened quickly after. The Mayor's panicked voice came filtering out of a phone speaker into the hall as the Captain hurried out followed closely by the Police Chief. Daniel shut the chaos out, shoving past other cops as he climbed the stairs two at a time. He was one of the first to come bursting into the interrogation room, coming face to face with Todd, face red and splotchy bruises forming around his neck where he was rubbing profusely. Next to the door an officer lay unconscious, slumped over at an awkward angle. At Todd's feet was another unconscious man in plain clothes, his face already swelling and turning purple.

"What happened?" Daniel asked, looking at the mess all around him. The hallway was already overrun with cops jockeying for entry into the room.

"Asshole tried to kill me," Todd answered, nudging the unconscious man a little too hard with his foot. Over the din of voices in the hall came the gruff commands of the Captain and Chief, demanding entrance. The other officers cleared out quickly enough, allowing the two men through.

Now Daniel sat in the Captain's office waiting for the Captain's return. The clock behind the sturdy oak desk read 30 minutes past midnight. This was bad. They needed to be mobilized as a team if they were going to save Kat. Instead, Daniel sat waiting like a kid in the principal's office. He bounced his leg in agitation. Unable to take it anymore, knowing Sadie was counting on him, he sprang from his seat, prepared to go when the office door came creaking open.

"Detective Guinto," the Captain said, voice clipped.

"Captain Davis," Daniel answered, keeping a tight control over his voice. "What's going on? We need to get to the train yard."

"Have a seat, Guinto," Davis said, brushing Daniel's concern off.

Daniel sat back in his chair, feeling stunned at the Captain's lack of concern. He watched him circle his desk before sitting nonchalantly in his expensive leather chair.

143

"Sir, what's going on?" Daniel tried again. Captain Davis regarded him coolly for a long moment before answering.

"EMTs came and checked your guy out. He's just waking up. We haven't questioned him yet."

"And Everett?" Daniel pressed, forgetting himself for a moment. The Captain paused, still examining Daniel, reading deeply into his frantic energy just beneath the surface.

"The EMTs gave him the all clear," Davis said, sitting back in his seat. "Look, I want you to keep an eye on our would-be assassin."

"What about the operation, Captain?" Daniel asked, disbelief coloring his face.

"That's well in hand." The Captain leaned forward in his chair, looking Daniel square in the eye. "You did really good work on this case. The Mayor is happy to put the terrorism question to rest. We'll get these guys in a cell soon."

"What about the girl?" Daniel cut him off, pointedly ignoring the Captain's raised eyebrow.

"Girl?" he asked, face blank.

"Kat." Daniel stood from the chair again.

"Oh. Everett's kid."

"Kat," Daniel repeated, fighting his agitation. "A person that needs our help." The Captain looked on blankly. Shaking his head Daniel composed himself. "Did you look her up at all? Her girlfriend is from the Dumont family. Jaime Dumont."

"The millionaire?" The Captain stiffened in his seat, suddenly fully alert.

"Yes," Daniel shot back.

"Why didn't you say anything sooner?" Davis stood reaching for the phone receiver on his desk.

"I didn't think I needed to convince you to do your job."

The Captain bristled but didn't respond. Instead, he sat the phone back down. "Go. Go get in a car with the other boys. Make sure she's safe." The Captain shoved him out of the office, picking up the phone again and dialing a number as Daniel shut the office door behind himself.

Headlights cut through the dark night, the glowing beams cast through the chain link fence illuminating slivers of the night. Sadie fought against the frigid air, hating the cold settling into her bones as she stayed crouched behind storage containers, clinging to shadows. Her ribs ached, sending ripples of renewed pain through her with every breath. She ignored the pain, instead focusing on the sound of an ancient motor sputtering to life, struggling under its task as it slid the chain link fence open. The motor was so ancient it took a solid five minutes to fully open allowing the vehicle in. It gave

Sadie enough time to slowly maneuver from her hiding space just enough to catch a glimpse of the newcomers. From her distant vantage point across the yard she could make out an old dented brown car. The headlights shined against the night keeping her from seeing its passengers. She tucked back into the shadows fighting her curiosity. It had to be them. The shoddy motor stopped. Then the sound of a car engine came bouncing off shipping containers and old trains. The motor sputtered again as it shut behind them. The car was getting closer. Holding her breath Sadie leaned out again just as the car passed by her hiding spot. Through the rear window Sadie caught a glimpse of auburn hair, an achingly familiar face. Kat. She wanted to scream, and cry, and collapse all at once. Instead, she kept her watch, staying deathly still till the car had passed out of sight behind a string of buildings sandwiched next to a row of shipping containers. She waited, straining to hear the car's engine, but nothing came. The quiet stretched over the yard. It frightened Sadie. She shoved it down alongside all her pain. With a steadying breath she stepped out of the shadows. Crouching low she quickly navigated a path, staying out of sight, stepping as lightly as possible, making herself invisible. Sadie rounded the building from the opposite side that the car had gone.

Reaching the edge of the dilapidated warehouse, still clinging to shadows, she caught sight of the car again. They had parked facing away from her, the nose of the car pointed north. Sadie conjured the train yard map in her mind. They were facing the direction Todd would be coming from. The yard was bisected by row upon row of train cars and shipping containers. The place was mostly dark. It was a deep, moonless night. Storm clouds were drifting in from the horizon. The few light posts in the yard were mostly dead and broken, at times sending flickers of light into the night before fading away again. From her new vantage point she could make out Vince and Jimmy in the front talking. Vince sat in the passenger seat with Jimmy behind the wheel. Kat sat in the rear. She was still while her captors spoke, each gesturing to the other. Suddenly their posturing ceased, the car shifting as both men turned to look at Kat. She could see their faces now, both perturbed. Sadie retreated around the corner, firmly out of sight, but unable to see. She fought every instinct to look, wanting to see Kat, know she was safe. The distinct sound of car doors opening followed by boots hitting gravel came from their direction.

"Asshole," Kat's voice cut through the night before the car doors were shut again. Sadie smiled to herself at the familiar voice, still full of fight.

"He's not here yet," Jimmy's voice rang out across the train yard.

"I know," Vince answered, tone neutral as if he were commenting on the weather. "Not like Todd's known for his punctuality."

Outside the train yard, Eddie sat in his car, parked not very far from where he'd let Sadie out. His car window was open despite the cold. He wanted to hear. His ears strained against the silence, listening for any sign of distress. Whatever was going on it was bad. He just knew. In the distance, he heard the sound of car engines approaching. Unusual in the desolate night. He sank down into the driver seat, disappearing from sight. A long row of black cars came inching steadily down the street. As they passed his car, scarcely paying him any mind, he noticed a half-busted, rusted out car, out of place among the obvious undercover cop cars. The string of cars stopped ahead of him, pulling to the side of the street and parking in orderly fashion. Once all the cars settled two men stepped out. One opened the back door letting out a middle aged red headed man. The man reluctantly got out, his face was tired, pinched and aggravated. The other man rounded the car, opening the trunk and producing two large black bags. The man reluctantly handed them to the red headed man who accepted them. They walked to the next car, a younger man exited the driver's seat, engine still running. He opened the trunk for the others before Red deposited the bags. Eddie strained to hear their conversation but caught nothing but garbled voices.

"You know what you're doing?" Daniel asked, squinting at Todd, scrutinizing the older man.

"Yeah, yeah. Make the exchange, don't get killed," Todd answered, shutting the trunk sharply and making for the driver seat. "Do you guys know what you're doing?"

"We'll be right behind you," Daniel said. The other cops eyed each other.

"Oh, good." Todd got in the driver's seat, shutting the door, and pulling out of the chain of cars. The other men stood silently staring at Daniel.

The car they gave Todd sputtered uncomfortably down the street jostling Todd in the driver's seat as it hit endless strings of potholes. Todd drove casually all the while griping to himself.

"This has been one of the more fucked up nights of my stupid fucking life." He shook his head, laughing sardonically. "My luck I'm gonna fucking die." He turned the car towards the gate Vince had told him to wait at. He had half a mind to turn the opposite direction and never stop running. But between Vince and Jimmy and the cops, someone was bound to shoot him. The drive to the gate was shorter than he would have liked. For long moments Todd sat in the car, watching the chain link fence. It wasn't too late to turn around. Flashes of Kat danced across his mind, the way she adored him when she was little. With a heavy sigh, Todd rubbed his sore neck, feeling the bruises softly. He put the car in park. Grasping the turn signal he flashed the headlights three times as instructed. He deliberately held the door's handle, taking a moment, scanning his surroundings before hesitantly stepping out the car. He waited what felt like forever in the cold, feeling it already settling deep into his skin, slipping under his light jacket. He resisted the slight itch where his wire was taped to his chest.

"What a shitty night," he groaned to himself.

Across the yard, Vince caught the flickering glow of the headlights illuminating the metallic wall of shipping containers in quick bursts.

"That's my cue," Vince said. Taking one final glance at Kat chained in the backseat he stopped himself. "Stay close. And don't do anything dumb." Jimmy huffed, watching Vince disappear out of sight. He turned back watching Kat rubbing at her wrists in obvious discomfort.

Todd watched the gate sputter to life before opening slowly. He slid back into the warmth of the car, shutting the door sharply and taking it out of park. He eased the rusted clunker through the entrance and into the train yard. In the distance, he spotted Vince illuminated in his headlights. For a moment Todd entertained the idea of flooring it, barreling over Vince in a metal ball of fury. He shook his head, seriously doubting this car could pick up enough speed to get the job done.

Todd eased the car into the agreed meeting spot, throwing it into park and cutting the engine he stepped out into the cold night. Vince steadily walked towards him.

From a distance, Sadie could faintly make out the sound of a car engine stopping, a car door shutting. She stayed glued in place watching over Kat diligently. After a moment Jimmy got back into the driver's seat. Sadie swallowed. It'd be really shitty to get run over twice in a day. She breathed deeply fighting the sharp pain in her ribs. Jimmy seemed to immediately preoccupy himself with Kat. He rolled the driver's window down, lighting a cigarette with the other hand. The smell of burnt tobacco drifted to Sadie, along with it Kat's voice, in obvious distaste over the smell. Sadie wanted to laugh. Jimmy snapped back at Kat. While they were distracted she mapped out all the possible paths to the car without being detected. She freed the gun from her waistband feeling the heavy weight of it in her hands.

She was lucky. Jimmy seemed plenty distracted by Kat's banter. She kept low to the ground, staying in the ample darkness, using every shadow and corner as cover. Finding purchase on the opposite side of a train car Sadie waited. She was as close as she could be without losing her advantage. Jimmy and Kat's chatter came to a brief pause when Jimmy turned to look out the passenger window. This was Sadie's shot, maybe her only. She stepped from the shadows just as Kat turned to look her way. Her face paled as recognition dawned on her features. Sadie held up one hand pressing a single finger to her lips, quietly asking for silence. Very slowly Kat nodded, only once before turning her attention back to Jimmy, still staring out the passenger window. The black cat from earlier came skittering out in a flurry of fur and growls as it wildly chased a group of fleeing rats . Jimmy looked on, mild disgust and curiosity set into the lines of his face.

Sadie moved as quick and as quiet as she could force her damaged body. She cleared the distance in moments and in one swift move pressed the barrel of her gun through the open car window into the back of Jimmy's head, pressing the barrel as hard as she could into his scalp.

"Hey Jimmy," Sadie said, feeling the tension take over Jimmy's body through the gun. "Why don't you stay real quiet and take a step out this car."

"What the fuck," Jimmy whispered to himself, shooting a dirty look at Kat before slowly turning to face Sadie. "Of fucking course," he huffed, deliberately reaching for the door's handle, Sadie's gun still inches from his face.

"Kat," Sadie said, never taking her eyes off Jimmy's every move.

"Hey," Kat said, a voice laced with fear that hadn't been there before. "What are you doing here?"

"Getting ready to shoot Jimmy I guess," Sadie answered. "Get on your knees," she directed Jimmy as he slid out the open car door. "Are you okay?" Sadie asked Kat, the edges of vulnerability creeping into her voice. "He didn't-they didn't-"

"I'm okay," Kat said, quieting her fears. Jimmy watched Sadie intently, waiting for any chance. Sadie never took her eyes away, keeping her pistol trained on him.

Separated by rows of rusted out train cars and metal containers Vince and Todd stood eyes fixated on one another.

"Stay right there!" Todd shouted, standing behind the open car door, the small barrier making him feel just a little safer. Reaching back into the beat up car he pulled on the trunk's latch and waited to hear the telltale click of its opening but nothing came. "Damnit!" he muttered, pulling it over and over till eventually it came open with a popping sound. Vince watched, exasperation settling onto him quickly,

"Are you fucking kidding me!" He gestured with his hands in frustration. Todd backed away along the car's side and pulled the trunk open in one move, pulling both bags out.

"Where's my kid?" Todd asked, slinging one bag on his shoulder.

"She's safe. And close. So just give me the fucking shit!" Vince shouted, radiating anger.

"I need to see her, Vince. How do I know I can trust you?"

"You got some fucking nerve," Vince answered. "I trust your dumb ass and look what it got me. Do you have any idea what you've done!?"

"Sorry?" Todd shrugged innocently.

"You're really lucky I'm not killing you right now," Vince said, starting to walk forward again. Todd instinctively took a step back.

"That doesn't exactly fill me with confidence," Todd replied.

"Fuck you!" Vince approached the car shoving Todd against it.

"Hey!" Todd yelled as pain shot through him at the impact. Vince held him in place by the collar and punched him once, sharply in the nose. "Fuck!"

The scream echoed through the yard colliding against metal surfaces only to reverberate back drawing Sadie's rapt attention away from her hostage, if only for a moment. Jimmy took that opening and in one swift move he came crashing into Sadie, launching himself clear into her center, sending the pistol flying out of Sadie's grasp.

All the air came bursting out of Sadie's lungs leaving her

breathless. Jimmy landed squarely on top of her, his large frame pressing her into the gravel under them. Kat screamed from the car, struggling against her restraints bolted into the car's floor. The metal bit into her skin, cutting hard where it came in contact. Before Jimmy could get off another hit Sadie had managed to bring her knee up between them, catching Jimmy sharply between the legs, causing him to pale as the world spun around him. Sadie scrambled out from under him and with another fierce kick she caught him in the jaw sending him falling face first to the ground. She forced herself to her feet, eyes searching frantically for the gun. Jimmy launched himself at Sadie again, his broad shoulder smashing directly into her fractured ribs. Sadie let out a guttural scream.

In the car, Kat fought frantically against the restraints making her wrist bleed as she used all her strength to pull at them. The metal looped into the welded hook began to give, coming out of place under her.

Jimmy grabbed Sadie and threw her against a rusted train car. She struggled against his hold. He threw a quick jab into her ribs watching intense pain cross her face. Sadie gasped feeling the sharp cracking of her rib.

"I'm glad it fuckin hurts!" Jimmy said, preparing to land another punch. From behind him a blow from a blunt object ricocheted off his skull. His eyes crossed before he collapsed, letting Sadie go, sending her crumbling in a heap to the ground beside him.

Kat stood over his limp body, a lead pipe poised above her head, clutched between two shackled hands, blood dripping down her wrists, poised to strike again. When he failed to move Kat dropped the pipe sending it clattering to the ground before she rushed to Sadie's side.

Sadie took in ragged breaths, each one more painful than the last. Her vision clouded with dizziness. She felt close to passing out, unconscious beside Jimmy.

"Sadie," Kat said, carefully cradling Sadie in her arms, keeping her as still as possible, inspecting her wounds. "Are you okay?"

"W-we need to get out of here," Sadie stammered, feeling consciousness begin to slip from her grasp. "B-before the cops sh-show up."

"Okay." Kat nodded, fighting back tears. "Can you walk?"

"I'll need help." Sadie forced herself to sit up in Kat's arms. The first drops of rain broke free from the sky and with a clap of thunder began to fall slowly then fast, one after the other. Sadie slung an arm over Kat's shoulder. Together they slowly stood, Sadie gritting her teeth to bear the sharp pain lancing through her.

"Maybe we shouldn't move you," Kat said, an arm wrapped tight around Sadie's waist.

"I'll be fine. Just get me out of here," Sadie said, "Asshat could wake up any second."

Kat nodded and against her better judgment began to walk

supporting Sadie's weight as they moved slowly across the yard. For a moment she wondered how her dad was fairing. The rain came down heavy on them as they moved slowly.

"Where do we go?" Kat asked, voice shaky as she tried not to jostle Sadie any more than necessary. The pain written on Sadie's face threatened to shut Kat down.

"There's a hole in the fence."

The walk was slow and painful. Kat carrying Sadie the whole way, so focused on her task she didn't notice the blood dripping from her wrists staining Sadie's clothes or the pain shooting up her arms. Outside the broken and bent bit of fencing Sadie finally collapsed, close to unconscious.

"I need to go back to the hospital," Sadie said, finally falling unconscious. On the other side of the fence, a car's headlights approached casting long shafts of light in the pelting rain. Kat climbed through the hole waving the car down. It came to a screeching halt beside her. The door clicked open and out stepped Eddie, his towering figure menacing in the dark.

"Eddie!?" Kat said, recognizing him immediately. "What are you-" she cut herself off, shaking her head in disbelief. "I need your help! Sadie, she's hurt!"

"Where is she?" Eddie walked to where he'd seen Kat crawl out.

"Through there." Kat followed him close. "I think it's her ribs."

Eddie nodded, climbing through the fencing. On the other side, he found Sadie sopping wet and unconscious, looking small and helpless. He checked her pulse. Still going strong. He gently lifted her into his arms and carried her back out into the world. Kat was waiting on the other side for her. Nearby sirens began to wail, flooding the night, turning pools of rainwater red and blue.

Chapter Six

It was peak summer, the shifting heatwave the city was thrust into could attest to that. It'd just turned August. Sadie would be starting 1st grade soon, but for now, that wasn't any concern to her. It was summer and like usual Sadie was all alone. It had been one year since her mom had gone. Her father was usually at work. He worked three jobs now. And when he wasn't working she didn't know where he was. But he certainly wasn't home. Oftentimes he'd stumble home in the night smelling funny and acting strange. She'd already mastered microwaves and frozen dinners.

Today Sadie was on her own. It was just after noon and she'd finished her peanut butter and jelly alongside some pudding and felt ready for an adventure. All she could think was to make her way from the cramped apartment she called home down to the small playground that occupied a plot of land across the street. Maybe she could find some neighborhood kids who wanted to play. She hoped for it as she stuck on her velcro sneakers and locked the front door behind her. She had lived her whole life here so she was pretty accustomed to the regulars. On the elevator ride down she cycled through all the other kids she'd seen that could be there.

Crossing the busy street carefully at the crosswalk Sadie caught sight of the playground, growing excited at the prospects of the day. Making it to the edge of the park she noticed something off about her surroundings. The sharp smell of tobacco wafted through the sticky heat filling the park with the acrid scent. Sadie's dark eyebrows furrowed in curiosity. She scanned the playground seeking out what was so peculiar. Across the park she saw a woman with curled blonde hair stubbing out a cigarette on the little cement walkway before plucking a fresh one from the pack, placing it between brightly painted lips and lighting it, all while never stopping the excited chatter that poured out of her. She was sitting on a bench with two women Sadie recognized from the neighborhood, but not her building. The women nodded along interjecting here and there when they could.

Sadie's examination of the strange women came to a halt at the sound of footsteps falling hurriedly against the pavement. She turned quickly, catching sight of a little girl, running around laughing thunderously, auburn hair sticking out all over, wild, full of joy. Sadie smiled at the delighted sounds. It wasn't long before, in her inattention, the little girl caught her foot on the edge of a sandbox filled with wood chips. She came tumbling down on the adjacent asphalt scraping up the palms of her hands and knees, tearing the skin till streaks of blood came pouring. The women on the bench didn't seem to notice. The handful of other kids kept running around while the girl tried not to cry. Sadie didn't even think. She ran up to the peculiar girl wanting to help. She kneeled beside the girl who instantly looked up, locking eyes with Sadie.

"Hi, I'm Sadie," she said. "Are you okay?"

The girl sniffled, wiping a tear away with the raw palm of her hand, leaving a slight streak of blood across her face. She nodded sniffling again before speaking.

"My name's Kat." Then she smiled.

"Are you sure you're alright?" Sadie poked gently at Kat's bloodied knee making the girl wince. Sadie's dark eyebrows knit together, her mouth turning into a slight frown. "Sorry."

"It's okay."

"Maybe your mom has band-aids," Sadie said. Her own mother had never kept anything like that around but it seemed like what you were supposed to do. Kat nodded, getting up and running off to the crowded bench.

"I fell, Mom! Do you have any band-aids?" Her mom ashed her cigarette, taking a moment before acknowledging her daughter's sorry state and answering.

"You're okay. Run along and play. We're going home soon." Kat wiped her bloodied palms on her shorts before running back to Sadie. Her mother turned back to her companions. "You shouldn't coddle them too much. They'll turn soft."

They spent the next hour playing before Kat's mom called her away. Sadie fell asleep on that lonely night thinking about her new friend, hoping she'd see her again soon.

She came to in a flood of white that burned her retinas.

"Am I dead?" Sadie asked. There was a slight shifting beside her. When her vision was less blurry she looked to her side. Kat was curled into a ball beside her, half asleep.

"If you're dead I'm dead too," she mumbled, voice husky from sleep, eyes fluttering open to look up at Sadie.

"Not so bad. Eternity in a white room."

"I'm here," Kat sighed, very carefully shifting her body till she could sit up.

"I know," Sadie said, a small smile forming on her chapped lips. Kat leaned over her, still cautious with every movement as she softly kissed her forehead. Sadie felt her heart pound in her chest, felt the entire world still all around them at the gentle caress.

"Are you okay?" Kat whispered as she pulled away scanning Sadie's face, eyes large and filled with worry.

"Everything hurts," Sadie said with a small sardonic laugh.

"I think that means we're alive," Kat replied, still searching Sadie. "I'll go get the nurse."

Sadie reached out placing a hand on Kat's arm, stopping her from leaving. Kat gave a slight wince of pain. Looking down she noticed the cuts and bruises along Kat's wrists. The skin looked angry and raw.

"What happened?" Sadie asked, moving her hand away quickly, afraid to hurt her again.

"I fractured my wrist," Kat said, holding up her other arm to show off the splint on it. "Cut them both up really badly too. How 'bout you?"

"I got hit by a car," Sadie replied with another sardonic laugh. Kat's face flooded with worry again. She started to move away remembering her mission to find a nurse. "Don't go."

"You broke a couple ribs," Kat said, tears forming in the corners of her eyes. "The doctors wanted to make sure your broken ribs didn't puncture an organ." She looked away.

"Hey," Sadie said, voice scarcely a whisper, "I'm tough. Besides, you saved me."

"From the mess I got you into."

"You didn't," Sadie said, quickly cutting her off. "I needed to keep you safe. I-" she stopped herself, shifting to sit up better, taking Kat's face in her hand forcing her to meet her gaze. " I missed you," her voice cracked. She leaned in pressing a searing kiss into Kat. "Okay?"

"I missed you too." Kat nodded, tears falling down her face. She kissed Sadie back, pouring everything into the contact, all the things she couldn't put into words.

A sharp rap at the door made them jump apart. Both women turned to look, spotting a nurse hovering in the doorway, closed fist still poised above the door's wood.

"Excuse me," the older woman said, giving a shy smile. "I'm Dorothy, your nurse Ms. Park. How are you feeling?" She eyed Kat with a knowing look. "You shouldn't be exerting yourself."

Sadie reddened at the comment. Kat turned away trying not to laugh.

"I'll give you two some privacy." Kat glanced at the nurse before kissing Sadie on the cheek and departing, maneuvering past Dorothy, still flush with embarrassment. Before she was out of sight she returned, head popping briefly back into the door, "I'll be back soon." She locked eyes with Sadie, an unspoken conversation passing between them. Sadie smiled nodding once. Kat smiled back and with a small wave she was gone.

Kat could hear Sadie talking with Dorothy, telling her she felt good considering the broken bits. Kat shook her head suddenly, painfully grateful Sadie was alive. She stopped in the hospital hallway amidst the humming fluorescents and people rushing. Leaning against a wall she closed her eyes, shutting the world out. Tears began to fall again and she hurried to wipe them away.

"Hey," a man's voice cut through the chaos pulling Kat's attention. She looked up to see Eddie standing there, hands tucked into his pockets looking almost embarrassed to be intruding. "You okay?"

"I don't know," Kat choked out. "I thought you left," Kat said, wiping the last tears away, trying to compose herself.

"Come here," Eddie said, stepping closer and opening his arms, he embraced Kat with a brief pat on the back. Kat sobbed harder. "What's up?" he asked, voice steady and calm.

"I'm such a piece of shit."

Eddie pulled away looking her in the eye. "Don't say that," he said sternly. "Everyone knows you're not."

Kat shook her head pulling away from Eddie. "What are you doing here?" She wiped at her face again.

"How's your knight in shining armor?" he asked.

"Sadie? She's hurt, but she'll recover," Kat sighed relief washing across her as her face and shoulders relaxed.

"That's good," Eddie said, keeping eye contact as he placed a hand on her shoulder.

"It's just-" Kat stuttered. "It's just my fault she's like that."

"I don't think you made her come to the rescue. In fact, she was quite adamant about getting you."

"What were you doing there?" Kat's mood turned hard at the reminder that Eddie met Sadie before. "The last time I saw you you were-"

"Working for Jaime," he interjected. "She called me. Said you were in trouble and your friend needed backup."

"Of course." Kat laughed, shaking her head. She took a step away from him.

"I'm sorry," Eddie said, shoulders slumped. "But I'm glad I was there. I don't apologize for that."

"I'm glad you were too," Kat sighed.

"I know it's not my business, but what happened between you and Jaime?"

"You're right, that isn't your business," Kat answered, turning to walk away.

"You were too good for her anyway."

"Thank you." Kat turned and looked back at him. "For helping Sadie. It…It means everything to me." She turned to go again.

"Hey," Eddie called, stopping her retreat. "If you ever need me… You know I'll be there, right? You were always such a good kid-"

"Thank you, Eddie," Kat cut him off sharply. She walked away leaving him awkwardly standing alone. For a moment he was at a loss. Shaking his head he snapped out of it and followed after her. He found her standing still in the waiting room staring at a nearby television, the local news flickering brightly across the screen. A photo of Kat at a gala with Jaime hovered above a news anchor's shoulder before changing to two mug shots. The captions underneath blurred by as the anchor droned on silently on the muted television. Kat turned to look at him as he stepped beside her. She looked utterly exhausted.

"Can I at least give you a ride home?"

"Okay," she said. "Just don't tell Jaime."

"Okay." Eddie nodded. "Want to get a coffee?"

"I should check on Sadie," Kat answered, arms wrapped around herself in the cold waiting room.

"Its only been a few minutes. The doctors are probably looking her over. Besides, I'm sure she could use some non-hospital food."

Kat nodded hesitantly, millions of thoughts racing through her head gave way to the practical notion Eddie offered. A small lifeline in the storm.

"There's a half-decent place across the street," Eddie said, giving her a gentle smile. He tilted his head towards the elevator banks. "We can be back real quick to check on Sadie."

Glancing towards the elevators Kat watched the silvery metallic doors slide open and Daniel step out. They locked eyes. Eddie followed her gaze till he noticed Daniel walking towards them.

"Kat," Daniel called to her. "Is she-"

"Yeah," Kat said. "She's awake. And with the doctor so maybe give her a minute."

"It's okay. I'm here as a friend." Daniel read her hesitancy. "I won't stay long. I have to get back to the station."

Kat scanned his face, the bags under his eyes, the ruffled hair and 5 o'clock shadow. "We're going to get coffee. Do you want one?"

"I'm okay," he answered. "Thank you." His words held an odd weight to them, out of place for a coffee run.

"Um," Kat began "How's Todd?"

"He's good," Daniel answered. "Safe. That's what matters most."

"Good," Kat answered, a small modicum of relief washing over her though she hardly knew why. After everything.

Daniel dug through his pockets till he produced a small slip of paper and passed it to her. A business card. "If you want to see him." She took the card carefully, holding it aloft between them. "Just give me a call."

"Thanks," Kat said, tucking the card away. She turned to Eddie. "Coffee?"

"Yeah," Eddie agreed. "Nice to meet you." He waved to Daniel as they turned to go.

They left Daniel in the waiting room scanning signs affixed to the walls till he saw what he was looking for. Following the painted arrow he went down the hallway till he found Sadie's room. Through the door he saw the doctor and nurse talking to Sadie. From the look on her face she wasn't terribly interested in what they had to say. After a few moments, the doctor and nurse left the room walking casually past him as they conversed. He slipped into the room.

"How you feeling?" he asked.

"Real tired of being asked that," Sadie responded without missing a beat.

"Maybe if you stayed out of trouble you wouldn't hear it so much," Daniel answered, only half joking.

"So you're saying I'm doomed?" Sadie asked.

"I guess that's up to you." Daniel entered the room and took a seat at her bedside.

"We'll see what happens." Sadie rolled her eyes. "I'm fine by the way. I mean I've been better, but I'll make it."

"Is that the official diagnosis?"

"More or less," Sadie replied shifting in her hospital bed, wincing at the traces of pain lacing through her beat up body.

"What brings you here?"

"Just checking up on you," Daniel answered.

"Well, mission accomplished. Though if you really wanted brownie points you woulda brought something chocolate."

Daniel chuckled, shaking his head. "Maybe next time."

"So what happened?" Sadie asked, turning serious.

"We arrested Vince and Jimmy. Todd's still in custody. He says he'll testify against them."

"Good." Sadie nodded.

"You shouldn't have left the hospital like that," Daniel sighed, fighting back his frustration.

"You're not going to make me regret it," Sadie said, shifting back into her pillows. "Kat's safe. That's what matters."

"Yeah."

Across the street Kat sat opposite Eddie in a little diner booth, sipping coffee while they waited for their to go orders. She couldn't help but look out the window every few minutes, eyes glued to the hospital, peering up to where she imagined Sadie's room to be. Eddie watched her freely while she was lost in her thoughts. He hadn't seen her in maybe 10 years. She was a girl then. Kat was so different now. All grown up, but more than that she looked exhausted. Beyond the hell of her last few days. She looked haunted. She looked weary.

"She's okay," Eddie said, drawing her attention away from the hospital window. "How have you been?"

Kat took Eddie in, fiddling idly with her coffee cup before taking a sip. Setting the mug back down she answered.

"I don't really feel comfortable telling you."

"Why?" Eddie asked voice even as he leaned casually against the enamel table top. "We used to be friends."

"Did Jaime pay you? To help me and Sadie," Kat clarified, still playing with the mug between her fingers, feeling its warmth seep into her.

"I would help even without getting paid," Eddie replied.

"Did she?" Kat pressed, holding his gaze, a steely edge lacing through her words.

"You know what Jaime's like." Eddie held his hands up in surrender. "And I need all the cash I can get."

"Okay," Kat sighed. "Thank you for your honesty." She took another sip of her coffee, enjoying the bitter taste, and glanced back out the window.

"So?" Eddie said, letting the unspoken question linger between them. Kat's gaze returned to him.

"I don't know what you want me to say. I've been through so much. And everything's so… different now." She looked hopelessly lost as she forced the words out.

"Okay. Um," Eddie sat thinking, eyes cast to the side while he considered his next words. "This Sadie, is she the same one you told me about before?"

"Yeah." Kat nodded before taking an idle sip of coffee.

"She's pretty." Eddie gave her that same easy familiar smile, sending Kat back to years ago when she was a teenage girl telling Eddie all about her best friend. "She's brave as hell too," he said, chuckling to himself between sips of coffee.

Kat laughed with him. "Yeah." Then with the warmest smile he'd seen from her since their reunion began, "She always has been."

"Pretty or brave?" Eddie asked, enjoying the dreamy expression Kat had fallen into.

"Both," she answered.

"I guess it's a good thing you guys are looking after each other."

"I don't know about that." Kat turned serious, though remnants of that warm glow remained.

"Why not?" Eddie asked innocently.

"Seems like I'm always hurting her. I never meant to but…it happens anyway."

Eddie shook his head dismissively. "You can't think like that. You'll talk yourself out of anything worthwhile if you do."

"That doesn't make me feel better," Kat answered, voice almost a whisper, nearly disappearing into the chatter of the restaurant's patrons. The waiter arrived carrying bags of food for them.

"Will there be anything else?" he asked politely.

"I think we're okay," Eddie answered, watching Kat recede back into herself. "Thank you."

They made the walk back to the hospital together. Eddie waited in the lobby till they needed him, leaving Kat to return to Sadie's room with her offering. She peeked through the glass door to see Sadie alone in the room, half asleep under the blankets. She didn't bother knocking. With her free hand she eased the door open, slipping inside and quietly shutting it behind her, trying not to startle Sadie.

"Hey," Sadie greeted, still reclined in the bed, her voice drowsy from sleep.

"I brought you things," Kat said, placing the bag on the small bedside table. "There's chocolate cake if you finish your dinner." She let out a small laugh.

"Is there really?" Sadie asked with a chuckle.

"Of course," Kat smiled. "Do you want to eat now or later?"

"Now is perfect," Sadie said, sitting up slowly. She was more awake now and couldn't help but stare at Kat now that she was back. "Thank you. For the food."

"It's no problem," Kat answered, watching Sadie closely.

"They said I can go home tonight."

"That's great." Kat gave a soft smile.

"Would you..."Sadie began uncertain how to ask for what she wanted. "I don't know what your plans are, um..."

Kat placed a comforting hand on Sadie's, running her thumb across the back of her hand. The small gesture quited Sadie's nerves. "It's okay, " Kat said.

"Would you stay with me? Just for a little bit." Sadie asked, looking deeply into Kat's eyes.

"You know I was going to anyway," Kat answered, her smile growing impossibly larger at Sadie's vulnerable embarrassment.

"Thanks." Sadie chuckled. "So what's on the menu tonight,

boss?"

Kat shook her head with a small laugh, opening the bag and handing Sadie a container. "Here." Sadie's fingers brushed against Kat's and lingered before she took the container and sat it in her lap.

"Hey," Sadie whispered, gently pulling Kat into a soft kiss. "Thank you."

"It's just food," Kat whispered back, brushing strands of Sadie's dark hair behind her ear.

"No way." Sadie smiled. The corners of her eyes grew damp. She tried to blink them away. "You saved me from hospital food." She laughed. Kat smiled, wiping away the faint traces of tears before pressing a kiss onto Sadie's soft lips.

"Go ahead and eat. Then we'll see about getting out of here."

"I can do that," Sadie said, giving Kat one more kiss before turning her attention to the take-out container. She was too tired to dwell on the millions of unanswered questions between them. For now, it was enough that Kat was close, that they were safe and together. After everything, she was too tired not to indulge in this intimacy she had always wanted with her. It was a funny paradox. Something she'd always dreamt about and she hurt so bad. The pain didn't matter though. Kat was here. At least for now.

Kat stayed close through the litany of paperwork and examina-

174

tions till hours had passed before the doctors finally let Sadie go. Dorothy had insisted she leave in a wheelchair. Hospital policy as she said. Sadie wasn't sure that was true. Kat had wheeled her out the front doors where Eddie was waiting in his taxi. He got out of the car to open the door and help Sadie in. Kat waved him off. She handed him a duffle bag with Sadie's things before taking her by the hand, helping her to slowly stand. With a slight wince, Sadie slid into the back seat. Kat shut her door and rounded the car getting in on the opposite side.

The car pulled away from the hospital joining the endless strings of traffic lined up, crisscrossing the city like blood surging through veins. The city was alive with people lost in the ebb of their lives, excited and hopeful for whatever comes next. Chasing after something. Whether they knew it or not. Kat slipped her hand into Sadie's, lacing their fingers together while they watched the world outside. Sadie leaned into Kat resting her head into her shoulder. Kat wrapped an arm around her carefully, holding her close while Eddie navigated the city, music softly playing from the cab's tinny speakers.

"I'm tired," Sadie said.

"We'll be home soon." Kat kissed her temple feeling the solid warmth of Sadie against her. The trip was a blur as they sat in their comfortable embrace. Soon Eddie's cab slipped from the stream of traffic to the side of the road not far from Sadie's front door.

"Do you need anything else?" Eddie turned around in the driver seat looking through the divider, eyes warm and eager to help.

"I think we're okay," Sadie answered, scanning the street out of habit. She turned her gaze to Eddie. "Thank you. For everything."

"It's no problem." Eddie gave a small nod. "Just take care of yourself."

"I'll try," Sadie answered with a sardonic laugh that made her ribs ache.

"Goodbye, Eddie," Kat said, stepping out of the car and retrieving Sadie's bag before opening the door and delicately helping Sadie out. Through the open door she said, "Try and take care of yourself too." He nodded again as he watched Kat shut the door. For a moment he watched the women slowly make their way to Sadie's building before a wave of exhaustion settled into him, the last day catching up with his weary body. He took off desperately wishing for his own home.

Outside the brick building, Sadie stopped them, glancing briefly at the apartment before looking to Kat. "Are you okay to go in there? A lot happened last time you were here."

"I'm fine," Kat answered. "Are you okay?"

"I mean it's home," Sadie said, fishing the building key from her pocket. She unlocked the door letting them inside. "Though I wish there was an elevator."

"We'll go slow," Kat said, helping Sadie through the small lobby and onto the stairs landing. Together they climbed step by step till they reached Sadie's door where just a few days ago they had been reunited. They'd both gotten so bruised in those short and intense days. Sadie slipped the key inside the lock noticing it had been fixed in her absence. "I think Daniel told your super to fix it," Kat said, noticing the curiosity pass over her face. "He seems to really care about you."

"He's a friend," Sadie answered. Turning the hall light on, Sadie scanned the small space.

"I think we're okay," Kat said, shutting the door and locking it behind them. She set Sadie's bag down on the nearby sofa. Sadie eased herself onto the couch, feeling the relief of sitting again. She struggled to take her jacket off without jostling herself too much while Kat looked on. With the first task managed she turned to her shoes. "Let me," Kat interrupted her, kneeling on the floor beside her. She gently removed each shoe, setting them aside, safely out of the way. "What do you want to do now?" Kat asked, still kneeling at Sadie's feet.

"A hot shower sounds good," Sadie sighed. "I just-"

"I'll help you," Kat said, cutting her off.

Sadie gave a devilish smile. "You sound a little eager," she chuckled.

"I just want to help," Kat smiled at her, eyes raking casually over Sadie's frame.

177

"Sure," she said, giving Kat a wink.

"Wait here," Kat said, leaning up to kiss Sadie sweetly. "I'll be back soon."

Then she was gone, disappeared to the bathroom to start the shower. Sadie smiled as she watched her go. She gave a slight shake of her head feeling a wave of sadness displace her. Maybe this was a bad idea. Maybe being so close would make it that much harder when Kat walked back out of her life. She swallowed down the fear. She started to feel, for the first time since their reunion, that maybe she couldn't let Kat go so easily this time. Her thoughts were interrupted by Kat's return.

"I think we're set," Kat said, approaching the sofa and taking Sadie's hand, helping her stand on her own two feet. With hands still entwined Sadie followed Kat into the bathroom.

The room was already warm and slowly filling with steam from the hot water pouring down in torrents. With nothing more than a look that communicated so much, Kat slowly began easing the clothes off of Sadie, first taking the hem of her t-shirt and lifting slowly revealing Sadie's soft skin. Goosebumps began to form immediately. Along her ribcage there was a motley of deep purple bruises spotting across her. Kat knelt before Sadie and delicately unbuttoned her jeans.

"Does that hurt your wrists?" Sadie asked, looking down at her, eyes large and expressive as she watched every movement Kat made, burning it into her memory.

"No," Kat answered simply. She grasped the waistband of Sadie's pants and slowly pulled till they were trapped around Sadie's ankles. "Lean on me." Sadie placed her hands on Kat's shoulders, slowly stepping out of the clothes, feeling exposed and vulnerable under Kat's heavy gaze. Kat met her eyes and saw the hesitancy. "Here," she said standing before Sadie. She stripped herself of her clothing till she was bared to Sadie. She took her by the hand leading them into the shower, letting Sadie lean against her as she struggled over the lip of the tub. Kat held her close, careful to not jostle Sadie too much. The hot water seeped into their skin, washing everything away from them. Kat reached for a loofah and soap, lathering it up before delicately washing Sadie.

"You don't have to," Sadie said.

"I want to," Kat answered, dropping a kiss on Sadie's damp shoulder. "Don't be afraid. I'm right here," she whispered. Sadie nodded slowly, savoring the feeling of Kat's hands tracing over her. She turned slowly, meeting Kat face to face, unable to stop, she kissed Kat slowly, a gentle burning caress that consumed them, shrinking their worlds down to the singular point where their lips met, blurring the lines between them. The kiss deepend till Sadie felt lightheaded. The dizzying feeling overwhelmed her, making her feel faint. She leaned heavier on Kat who clutched her tighter. "Are you okay?" She whispered, fear lacing through her voice.

"Yeah." Sadie fought the spell, grounding herself in Kat's arms. "I-I just need to take it slow." She gave a weak smile. Kat kissed her cheek.

"Do you want to get out of here?"

"No." Sadie clung to Kat under the water's heat. "Not yet."

Kat nodded. She continued passing the loofah over Sadie's skin letting the stream of water wash away the soap and dirt. She found a shampoo bottle on the ledge of the shower and took it, pouring out the soap and delicately beginning the process of washing Sadie's hair. Sadie watched her closely as she tended to her, the intense way she focused biting her lip softly as she went. Sadie shut her eyes, tipping her head back under the water, washing the shampoo away. When she opened her eyes Kat was watching her, large eyes burning into her, full of awe. Kat took the other bottle and began working the conditioner into Sadie's dark hair.

"What about you?" Sadie asked, finding the loofah and soap nearby. She took it and lathered it up again and began cleaning Kat in turn. Kat gave a low groan at the sensation giving Sadie pause. She took her gaze from her hands where she had traced each patch of exposed skin she touched to Kat's trying to read her expression. Kat bit her lip and sighed.

"It feels good when you touch me," Kat answered. "Sorry."

"Don't be," Sadie cut off her apology. She continued her task ignoring the excitement pooling low in her stomach. In turn, they finished washing till the water began to go cold. Kat got out first, getting the towels she'd left out earlier. She wrapped one around herself quickly before opening the other for Sadie who stepped into Kat's waiting arms. She held her delicately for a moment, both women savoring the comfortable quiet.

"C'mon," Kat whispered into Sadie's ear. Taking her by the hand she led them into the bedroom where she'd laid out pajamas. She indicated Sadie sit down on the edge of the bed. Sadie sat slowly, careful not to shift too much. Kat took the loose t-shirt she found and held it out for her, motioning for her to lift her arms.

"This is ridiculous," Sadie chuckled, taking the shirt from Kat's hands.

"You broke a rib. It's okay to need help," Kat said, taking the shirt back. She eased it onto Sadie being careful not to move too fast. "What's on your mind?" she asked, taking the shorts she'd laid out and helping Sadie into them.

"Um," Sadie paused. "I'm just tired," she said, glancing back at the bed. The last time she'd laid here with Kat had been very different and maybe just as intense.

"Let's lay down," Kat suggested. "I'm exhausted too."

Together they laid under the covers, heads resting side by side on the pillow, neither quite sure what to say. "Can I hold you?" Kat asked. "It's okay if you don't want that. I'd get it."

"Kat," Sadie answered, voice cracking. "Please," she said, drifting off, unable to find any words.

"Come here." Kat gently pulled Sadie closer into the protection of her arms. She kissed Sadie's temple feeling the other woman's breath even out as she surrendered to the heavy weight of sleep. Kat watched her sleep as long as she could, feeling a painful ache in her chest as she memorized Sadie's peaceful face, all the little ways she'd changed in those absent years. She felt so guilty just stepping back into Sadie's life, touching her like nothing had ever happened, picking up where they'd left off. Chaos and all. She couldn't help herself. She'd always been drawn to Sadie. Since the start. In all the ways they'd changed, that pull was something that remained, growing and transforming over and over again. She threw all that aside, too exhausted to dwell any longer. Right now was everything she wanted. She couldn't bear the thought of tomorrow.

She awoke to traces of sunlight fluttering into her eyes and Sadie peering up at her still resting quietly in her embrace.

"Good morning," Sadie said, smiling into Kat's neck.

"Hey," Kat mumbled, rubbing the palm of her hand across her face, rubbing the sleep from her eyes. "How are you?"

"I'm okay," Sadie answered into the quiet room. "A little achy. Kinda hungry."

"I can make us something," Kat said, suddenly feeling very awake. "Stay right here." She began getting out of bed, cautiously avoiding moving Sadie too much.

"I'll come with you," Sadie said, slowly following Kat out the bed.

"You should rest," Kat protested.

"I am." Sadie took Kat's hand and guided her to the kitchen. "What are you thinking?" Kat swallowed, staring at Sadie's innocent face in profile as she followed closely behind. Her mind flooded with thoughts and for a long while she was silent. "That hard a question?" Sadie looked over her shoulder with a quirk of her lips into a half smile and a playfully raised eyebrow.

"Sadie," Kat said, stopping in her tracks, making Sadie stop and wait for what Kat had to say. Kat lifted a hand to gently stroke Sadie's dark hair, looking into her big eyes. She kissed her softly, brushing her lips across Sadie's feeling her stomach tighten with the rush of feelings tangled together. The small favor quickly silenced the avalanche in Kat's head. She pulled away gently brushing the tip of her nose against Sadie's "Let's see what's in the kitchen." She kept hold of Sadie's hand as they entered the small room. Reluctantly she let it go and moved to the fridge where she started rifling for ingredients. "Should probably get some groceries soon."

Sadie leaned against the countertop carefully finding a stance that didn't hurt. Having Kat nearby helped distract her from the discomfort. After breakfast she'd have to take the pain pills the doctor had given her which would probably put her out of commission. She hated feeling helpless. She watched Kat fuss over food, mumbling to herself as she figured what to make. She wondered what had passed through Kat's head in the hallway. Probably the same things that had kept her awake the night before.

"How'd you sleep last night?" Sadie asked.

"Okay, I guess." Kat smiled half-heartedly.

"Just seemed like you were up late."

"Yeah," Kat replied, idly playing with a carton of eggs on the counter. The silence hung heavy between them.

"Is it Todd? You haven't gotten to speak to him yet."

"Oh," Kat said, looking up suddenly. "Daniel said he could help with that. He gave me his card."

"Are you going to call him?" Sadie asked, carefully reading Kat's expressions.

"Later," Kat said, finding a pan in the drying rack and placing it on the stovetop. "Everythings been so intense. I'm not ready yet"

Sadie placed a hand on Kat's shoulder interrupting her from her task. "There's no rush."

They shared a simple breakfast of eggs and toast and watched tv nestled into Sadie's living room sofa under piles of blankets, shifting into different positions throughout the afternoon into the evening, always remaining close, often touching. Simple gestures. Hands on knees, a touch of the shoulder, a caress on the arm, leaning into each other. As expected the painkillers made Sadie drowsy though she fought against it feeling determined to savor this small window of time before her friend disappeared from her again. The thought made her uneasy, but it could have been the pills. Interrupting the show that had been droning on was a news broadcast promoting tonight's segments. Kat's face fluttered across the screen and for a moment Sadie swore she'd hallucinated.

"Was that you?" she mumbled.

"Yeah," Kat huffed, changing the channel. "Its come on a few times now."

"I'm sorry," Sadie apologized without thinking.

"It's not your fault," Kat sighed, cupping Sadie's face in one hand. "Are you okay?"

"I think I need to sleep," Sadie answered.

"Want to go to the bedroom?"

"Yes," Sadie nodded, already half asleep.

Kat helped her up and to the bedroom, setting the other woman down on the mussed blankets they hadn't bothered to fix earlier. Sadie fell asleep immediately, scarcely noticing Kat adjusting the blankets all around her. Kat sat to one side watching the rise and fall of Sadie's chest, the way her face relaxed into a peaceful slumber. It made her heart ache. All those years of desperately wanting to be with no one but Sadie came rushing into her anew. On the nightstand her phone buzzed, the plastic rattling against the wood making a tinny sound. Kat rushed to silence the device, afraid of waking Sadie.

'I saw the news? Are you okay? Are you still in town?' A text illuminated the glass screen. Harvey McCormick. That was a name she hadn't thought of in ages. A decade ago he had been her closest friend at the private school Jaime had pulled strings to arrange her attendance at. They had bonded quickly over being gay and too afraid to expose themselves to the kids privileged enough to attend that place. People began to assume they were dating that whole year. They never corrected them. They even went to senior prom together.

'Hey, Harv! I'm fine. Yes, I'm in town for a while.'

A new message appeared in moments. 'Can we meet? It's totally okay if you're overwhelmed.'

'I'd love to. Maybe tomorrow.'

Kat sat the phone back on the nightstand among the things she'd pulled from her pockets before bed. Mixed in with the mess was Daniel's card. She plucked it from the pile, taking the phone back up as well. She scanned the phone number etched into the front for long moments. Making a decision she punched the number into the phone. With a deep breath, she settled on her words, quickly composing a message.

'Hi Daniel, It's Kat. I'd like to see my father.'

She placed the phone and card back on the nightstand. Stretching out on the bed beside Sadie, being careful not to shift around too much. In the darkened room she slowly drifted to sleep, the last thing she saw was Sadie's peaceful face, beautiful and serene, even in the shadows.

The next day Kat had reluctantly left Sadie's side to meet Harvey at his Manhattan office. Standing in the lobby on the 32nd floor she watched the city below through the office's tall windows that let daylight pour in bringing the place to life. Outside a milky fog had rolled in turning the world into an ominous dreamscape. She tried to remember why she had agreed to this.

"Kat," a voice came from behind her. She turned to see Harvey looking a world different from the teenage boy she had known. Still handsome but more filled out and muscular, not so lanky, and in an expensive suit tailored into a close fit, the dark blue color complimenting his dark brown skin. "How are you?" He smiled, opening his arms for a hug. He scooped Kat up into a brief embrace before releasing her. "Oh your poor wrist," he said, noticing the brace on her arm. "Did those monsters do that to you?"

"Um," Kat said, already overwhelmed.

"Sorry," Harvey answered, stopping himself. "I'm glad you're here."

"Me too." She smiled half-heartedly.

"Let's catch up over lunch. On me." Harvey smiled wider leading her to the elevators. He had chosen an elegant cafe for their meal. They sat across one another in the restaurant's warm glowing lights sipping overpriced coffees and waiting for their meals to arrive.

"It's amazing that you're working for Williamson. They're one of the best agencies right now."

"We've had quite the boom," Harvey said. "And you're-"

"Doing PR out in L.A.," Kat answered. "For GCI."

"Impressive." Harvey raised an eyebrow. "You know, I don't know if you've ever thought about moving back, but Williamson is opening a new PR branch and we're looking for top talent to spearhead."

"Oh?" Kat's head tilted curiously as she listened. "I'd have to think it over. Maybe get some details first."

"Of course. I'll have someone reach out to you." Harvey searched her face, feeling happy to be with an old friend.

"Thank you." Kat reached out briefly touching his hand. Her phone buzzed inside her purse interrupting the moment. "Sorry," she said, sheepishly reaching for the device. "It might be an emergency." Meaning Sadie could need her. Harvey waved a hand for her to take it just as the waiter arrived with two plates balanced in hand. Digging her phone out she saw a text notification illuminated on the screen. Daniel. She opened the message.

'Sorry for the short notice but can you meet me at the police station? In a couple hours. I'll take you to see Todd.'

A sharp knock at the door pulled Sadie's attention from her daydreams and inner thoughts turning inwards on themselves. The television droned quietly in the background, the half-muted voices keeping Sadie company. Kat had been gone a few hours now. It was the first time Sadie had to think when the world wasn't on fire. So far the time alone had only created more questions and not an answer in sight. She looked to the front door hearing the knock come again. It couldn't be Kat. She had given her a key before she left. Kat had given her a strange look she couldn't quite place before kissing her softly, letting the connection go on for a small forever before taking her leave, going on about how she didn't want to be late. It was so bittersweet. The old stirrings of love awakening in every fiber of her paired with that painful stabbing ache, not trusting this was real in any context. Soon she'd be gone and this would become a distant hazy dream to clutch on to.

Sadie took painful steps to stand and walk to the door. The knock came again. Through the peephole she caught a familiar face, Andy. She smiled in relief, unlocking the door quickly and pulling it open.

"Andy!" Sadie greeted, a smile illuminating her face.

"Are you okay?" Andy asked, bypassing the formality and letting herself into the apartment. Sadie shut the door behind her, locking it once again. "I saw your friend on the news. I figured if she was in trouble you were probably half dead trying to get her out of it."

"I'm fine," Sadie answered a little hesitantly, "A broken bone, some scrapes and bruises, but nothing that won't heal."

"And Kat?"

"A fractured wrist. But she's fine. She's safe."

Andy took her jacket off resting it on the sofa's arm. "What'd you break?"

"My ribs," Sadie sighed, hating the pain emanating from her torso.

Andy's face pinched with worry. She went to Sadie scanning her. "Are you sure you're fine?"

"I'm trying," Sadie answered, searching Andy's warm dark eyes.

"Where's Kat? Back in L.A.?"

"She's visiting a friend, but she'll be back later."

"She's staying here?" Andy's eyebrows raised in surprise. "How'd that happen?"

"I don't know. I...I just feel better with her here," Sadie answered, eyes watering. She looked down, unable to look at Andy.

"Is that okay? To just let her back into your life, like nothing happened."

"I can't help it." Sadie felt the first tear fall. She took a deep breath releasing it slowly. "It's like… like I can't control myself, like I can't stop indulging *this*."

"And when she leaves?" Andy couldn't help but ask, reaching out and delicately wiping her tear away.

"I can't think about that right now." Sadie shook her head. Andy took her delicately into her arms, cradling Sadie gently.

"Have you talked to her about any of this?"

Sadie stood silent a moment in Andy's embrace before pulling back. Andy dropped her arms, letting go. "And say what?"

"I don't know. How you feel?" Andy looked Sadie over, stepping away she took a seat on the sofa's arm. Sadie was silent. Andy waited, but nothing came. "Do you know how you feel?"

"Well…kind of. It's complicated."

"Why? Cause of all the stuff with Todd?" Andy started to feel a peculiar worry in her gut as Sadie seemed to flounder for answers.

"No. We…" Sadie trailed off looking at her feet. "We had sex."

"Oh," Andy said, face blank, eyes wide as she processed the implications. "Oh." Silence hung heavy between them, the sounds of city life below occasionally breaking through. "So you two are just what? Playing house right now?"

"I can't-I can't help it," Sadie sighed, running a hand through her hair and pacing the floor, ignoring the discomfort radiating through her torso.

Andy took a deep breath, letting the air fill her before letting it go in one big exhale. "So…how do you feel about it? Don't tell me you don't know, 'cause I know you do."

"I don't want to think about it," Sadie said, stopping her pacing in front of her window.

"Sadie?" Andy pressed, standing again and moving behind her. She placed a comforting hand on her shoulder. Sadie turned to face her.

"I still love her," Sadie whispered, tears falling from her eyes. "I missed her."

"She doesn't have to be gone forever. I'm sure you guys can figure something out," Andy said, eyes growing damp as she watched Sadie in pain. The pit in her stomach only seemed to grow.

Not far from Sadie's apartment a taxi pulled outside the police station double parking long enough to let Kat out. She reached back in through the open passenger window handing the man the fare along with a generous tip.

"Thank you," she said, he gave her a large smile revealing rows of crooked teeth. He pulled off leaving her alone on the sidewalk, staring down the police station, unsure of how to proceed. Before she could scrounge together a plan in the tangled confines of her mind, something she utterly failed to do on the long car ride, she spotted Daniel. Coming through the station's front doors by himself and jogging quickly down the stairs right in her direction. He didn't bother with a greeting, instead he waved for her to follow him all the while nervously eyeing their surroundings. She followed him, swallowing down the sudden onset of anxiety.

"Hey," Daniel finally said as they approached his car. "Sorry for the rush. We shouldn't linger here. Press has been hanging around a little too much and I think the Chief is a little too eager to get a photo op with our rescued victim."

Kat nodded along. "Where are we going?"

Daniel unlocked the car, opening the driver side door. "To see your dad." Kat opened the passenger door climbing in beside him. "He's in holding not far from here, but seeing him is going to be complicated. For a while. So this is kind of…off the record. So to speak. I'd appreciate it if you didn't-"

"Tell anyone about this?"

"Yeah." He nodded with a sigh, both hands gripping the steering wheel. He hadn't started the car yet. "Except Sadie. I guess that's fine."

Kat nodded. "You two are really close, huh?"

"I worry about her," Daniel said. He put the key in the ignition, sending the engine roaring to life.

"Me too." Kat watched him closely, the way his jaw set as he focused on the road, mind clearly elsewhere.

"I know. I can tell."

The detention center was vastly different than she had expected. It was a squat brick building that seemed older than everything around it by decades. Inside reminded her of a hospital with its sterile hallways and fluorescent lights casting everything in a sickly glow. She followed Daniel closely through winding corridors as they were waved through back doors, avoiding security checkpoints. They didn't speak as they moved through the building, scarcely noticed till they reached an unremarkable door. A guard stood outside waiting. When he saw them he approached, stride stern and all business.

"This her?" the man asked, eyeing Kat before looking to Daniel.

"Yeah." Daniel nodded. "Thank you."

"Don't take too long," the man said, meeting Kat's eyes. A look of empathy passed between them. "Dan you gotta go. I'll escort her out when she's done."

"What? We didn't-"

"Go in the room with her or go. You can't be seen here."

"I'll be fine," Kat said, nodding to Daniel. "I promise."

Daniel nodded back. The guard waved for Kat to follow him. He scanned the hallways before opening the door, letting Kat in. She stepped inside hearing the firm click of the door shut behind her.

Sitting at the table in an orange jumpsuit, haggard and bruised was someone she hadn't laid eyes on in 18 years. Todd Everett.

"Hey." He waved with that same charming smile she remembered. She wanted to cry. Her stomach tightened in knots till she wanted to vomit. "Figures the next time you see me I'm in jail."

"You look like shit," she laughed, trying to keep her grasp on reality.

"I know. I'm an old man now." Todd chuckled.

"No. Your face. Did Vince do that to you?" she asked, eyeing the yellowing swollen bruises dotting his face.

"Some of it. Hey, you wouldn't happen to have any smokes?"

"I don't smoke anymore," she answered, looking embarrassed.

"It's a good thing," Todd said. "Sit." He waved to the chair opposite him. "How've you been?"

"It's been real shitty," Kat sighed, staring at her father unsure if he was real.

"You're telling me," he huffed, running a hand through his thinning hair.

"Dad. W-what happened?"

"Kind of a loaded question." Todd tilted his head giving that same grin. "Could you be more specific?"

"Was stealing the drugs your plan?" Kat asked, voice serious, cutting through Todd's playfulness. Her stomach turned again recognizing herself in the near stranger that was her father.

Todd shifted in his chair sitting straighter than before. "You know, that wasn't the question I thought you'd ask."

"What did you think I'd ask?" Kat squinted as she watched him closely, trying to read every microexpression that crossed his face.

"Where'd you go? Why'd you go? That sort of stuff."

"Well?" Kat asked, waiting for any answer Todd had to offer for any of his messes. He only sat quietly, tired eyes searching her face, committing it to memory.

"Wow," he said, breaking the silence. "You're so big. All grown up. You know you look so much like my mother. When she was your age of course. I don't think you ever saw any photos of her when she was younger."

"Dad." Kat stopped him.

"Right," Todd answered, snapping out of his daze. "Answers. To which question?"

"Any," Kat pressed.

"I left because I had gotten in some trouble and your mom and me hadn't gotten along in years. I figured you'd be okay without me. Wasn't like I was a great dad when I was there."

Kat shook her head letting a sardonic laugh slip out. "Fuck you." She laughed again, fighting off that queasy feeling.

"Yeah. I get that," Todd answered.

"You have no idea how much worse everything got when you left."

"What? Your mom had some shitty boyfriends?"

"Tommy moved in."

Todd turned quiet, sobering to the realization. "Why would

she do that? She knows Tommy's messed up."

"No fucking kidding." Kat shook her head, wiping away the errant tear falling down her face. Meeting Todd's steely gaze, she caught a flash of anger quickly beaten back.

"Are you okay?"

"Probably not," Kat answered. The door creaked open behind Kat. She turned to the intrusion.

"Hurry it up," the guard said, poking his head in for only a moment before retreating.

"Will I be able to see you again?" Kat asked, not sure what she wanted the answer to be.

"Probably not. Part of this whole deal is that I go into witness protection after I testify." Kat's brow furrowed at the revelation. She felt the air leave her lungs and for long moments she couldn't fathom the next breath. "Look, I need to talk to you about something really important. That number I gave you-"

"That lady," Kat said, lost in a daze.

"What? No. Your brother. Jason."

"What?" Kat asked, snapping out of it. "Who?"

"Your brother." Todd raised his eyebrows confused about her stupor. "Jason. I know I'm no good, but you should get to know him. Look out for him. Someone has to."

"How do I-"

"Just call the number back. Tell Mary Ann to stop messing around and let you talk to Jason. It's important."

The door opened again, this time the guard stepped inside. "We have to go," he said, face apologetic as he looked at Kat.

"But," Kat said, realizing there was nothing she could do to make this moment longer. "Dad?"

"There's time. Before the trial. Try to come back," he said, standing with her. "Try to call." He scooped her into his arms before she could think, hugging her tight. She felt dampness against her head. Todd was crying. The guard nodded to the door, signaling it was time. Todd released her reluctantly before she was whisked out of the room, the door shutting firmly behind her.

Kat stumbled into Sadie's apartment scarcely remembering how she got there. Only the vague notion of Daniel driving her back to Sadie's without asking where she wanted to go. Now she stood poised in the doorway in a quiet, darkened apartment unsure of what to do. For long moments she stood there trapped in her daze, the whole day swirling on the surface of her brain, still far from sinking in. Still miles away from the incoming fear and doubt, anger and confusion. Mostly she felt tired. Suddenly she noticed she was still lingering in the open doorway and shut the door, locking it tightly behind herself. She set her bag down and slipped her jacket off, tossing it onto the nearby sofa like she was coming home from a tumultuous work day. She bypassed everything heading right for the bedroom. The door was still open and inside was Sadie, stretched out, asleep in her bed. Watching Sadie, suddenly all the thoughts drifted away and all that was left was them, alone, together in a room. She felt like crying again. Kat undressed in the dark, slipping her clothes into the laundry basket, unsure why she so desperately wanted to live in this pretend life. Playing along with all the things that never were. Maybe they still could be. After all, here she was arriving 'home' late at night to a sleeping lover. She approached the bed, careful not to wake Sadie as she pulled the blankets back, slipping under the covers. Sadie slid closer on instinct, pulling Kat into her, eyes still shut.

"You're back," she whispered, voice laced with sleep, the words half relief, half wonder.

"Of course," Kat answered. "Go back to sleep." She leaned down pressing a kiss onto Sadie's lips. She kissed her back carefully, chasing Kat when she pulled away.

"I missed you." Sadie's eyes were open and in the dark she peered deeply into Kat.

"I missed you too." Kat felt completely exposed under Sadie's gaze and too tired to lie.

"How was today?"

Kat didn't have an answer for her. Every moment of the day came colliding into her all at once till it drowned her and all she could do was cry in Sadie's arms letting her teardrops fall onto exposed skin. Sadie sat up, suddenly awake with worry.

"Are you okay?" Sadie traced a hand along her face. Kat shook her head, still crying, unable to speak. Sadie pulled her closer. For a long time Kat cried in her arms while Sadie stroked her hair, patiently waiting. Slowly her sobs passed and the room fell to complete silence, Kat's breathing evening out to a steady rhythm. Sadie kissed her forehead and wiped away the last of her tears. It hurt so much watching Kat fall apart like that. Living with that impossible helplessness where all she could do was hold her and wait. It was enough just to let Kat know she wasn't alone. Not ever.

When Andy had left Sadie had been exhausted from her aching ribs and the frantic emotions surrounding the last few days. She had taken her pain meds and laid in bed hazily pondering over the mad tangle of feelings she had for Kat. The love that was surprisingly strong after all this time, like she had merely been on pause, a part of her always waiting to resume. Then there was the fear. The absolute fear that soon Kat would be gone again, maybe forever this time. Then of course the anger, still somehow twisted in her gut. Part of her still felt this anger that Kat would crash back into her life, throwing everything into chaos only to walk away again. But then again… she didn't know that yet. And there was still this relief that washed away the anger, that Kat had come to her when the world was dangerous and everything was falling apart. That she still trusted her enough to let Sadie protect her. And above all else was the endless desire, the passion she still had for Kat. Even now. Raw and immediate and overwhelming. Kat was still so beautiful, and it caught her and held her and left her helpless to the chaos. She'd missed her so much. It all exhausted her. Sadie drifted to sleep and awoke to Kat crawling into bed and into her arms. Seeking shelter in her. And all the feelings melted away and all that was left was love. Watching her sleep she knew she was hopelessly lost. She fell asleep still holding on.

Hours later she woke to Kat watching over her, face contemplative as she took Sadie in.

"So you want to talk about it?" Sadie asked as if their conversation had never been interrupted.

Kat nodded, leaning down to kiss Sadie, taking courage from the simple touch. "Daniel took me to see my dad," Kat whispered into the room.

Sadie's brow furrowed. "Oh." She slowly sat up to meet Kat eye to eye. "So you're not okay." Kat shook her head stiffly. "How'd it go? What'd he say?"

"It was short. And intense," Kat answered, pausing to search for the right words. Sadie took her hand squeezing lightly, letting her know she was still there. "He said he was going into witness protection."

"Oh." Sadie's eyes widened.

"He said I had a brother. A half-brother. Jason. That I need to look after him."

"That's...intense." Sadie touched Kat's face, cradling her cheek in the palm of her hand. Kat leaned into it grateful for everything that was Sadie.

"Thank you," Kat whispered.

"What?" Sadie's brow furrowed with confusion.

"For letting me back in," Kat answered. "I don't think I could have done this without you."

Sadie leaned into her, though her body protested, and kissed Kat. "I wouldn't let you do it alone," she whispered, feeling Kat's warm breath against her lips. "What now?"

"I don't know," Kat said. "I need to go home eventually." Something flashed in Sadie's eyes, though she didn't say anything. "I don't know if I want to." Kat sighed. Sadie leaned in kissing her. "Sadie, what do you want? I don't-I don't have the right to ask for anything, but what do you want?"

"I just want you to be happy," Sadie answered, hating herself for not being selfish. Kat nodded with a sad smile.

"I want that for you too." She pressed a soft kiss into Sadie. "Can we go back to sleep?"

"Of course," Sadie answered, slipping lower into the covers with

Kat. "Kat?" she began still wanting to give voice to everything unsaid.

"Yes?" Kat mumbled, already falling asleep. Sadie watched her, eyes heavy lidded and drowsy.

"Goodnight," she said, nuzzling closer to Kat.

"Goodnight, my Sadie," Kat answered, voice heavy with sleep. Sadie stayed awake committing the fine details of this moment into her memory.

Morning came with sunlight spilling into the room, falling across Sadie's face and waking her to an empty room and empty bed, the blankets still crumpled and mussed where Kat had slept. Proof she was real. The door came creaking open revealing Kat carrying a tray laden with food, wearing a pair of Sadie's shorts and one of her old t-shirts, washed and worn soft over the years. She'd never looked so beautiful.

"Hey, sleepyhead," Kat said, setting the tray on the nightstand before climbing back into the bed. "I bet you didn't eat dinner last night."

Sadie shook her head. "I bet you didn't either."

"No," Kat grabbed a piece of toast, taking a bite and dropping crumbs all over.

"I think you're the only person I can tolerate bed crumbs for." Sadie laughed to herself. Kat blushed at the words, an uncharacteristic look for her. It reminded Sadie of the girl she'd been all those years ago. "Kat. I know everything's been so crazy, but…" Sadie drifted off searching for what she wanted to say. Kat watched her, waiting patiently. "I just, I hope you can…we can stay in touch. Be…have some kind of relationship again. Whatever that is."

For long moments Kat sat quietly. "Sadie I don't-I don't think it's a good idea for you to try and keep me around."

"W-why?"

"Look at the mess I made for you. In days." Kat looked away already feeling the prickling sting of tears in her eyes.

"That's not your fault." Sadie turned her head with a gentle touch and pressed her forehead against Kat, needing the closeness. "Do you know how much it hurt when you went away? How often I thought of you?"

"I do," Kat answered, voice heavy with that shared pain. "I probably thought of you everyday."

"Look, I don't expect for things to stay…like this, but I want to know you're okay. Can we do that?"

"Yeah, I think so," Kat said, giving a sad smile. "And I want to know you're okay too."

"I promise," Sadie said, kissing her cheek with the quiet words.

"I promise," Kat repeated, kissing Sadie's lips. "You should eat your breakfast."

Sadie smiled. "I will." And she kissed Kat again feeling a little less afraid.

It was maybe another week before Kat would fly back to L.A., back to the life she had put on hold for this complicated misadventure. And to what result? A father soon to disappear once again, a mystery brother she had somehow been tasked to look after. An old friend and the endlessly complicated relationship between them. Kat couldn't say she had come any closer to processing any of it in the week that passed. She'd stayed longer to look after Sadie. Just a little longer. And maybe see her father again. There were a lot of 'ifs', 'ands', and 'maybes', but she couldn't wait forever. Her life was waiting and with it the chance to get far enough away to sort her thoughts. Mostly everything up until the day she'd be leaving was filled with Sadie. Everything about her and Sadie frightened her. But locked away inside Sadie's apartment, in their own private world it just didn't matter. She didn't have any answers, but for now, she had this small sense of peace. For a week she found herself constantly staring at this girl she thought she'd lost. Memorizing everything she could. Etching bits of Sadie into herself. The way sunlight illuminated her face in early morning hours, catching on the curves and angles of her. The way she smiled and laughed as they stretched out on the sofa watching mindless tv side by side. Her smile always surprised Kat, the way it unfurled, slow at first then all at once. The most beautiful smile Kat had ever seen. Even to this day. She appreciated the slow days after everything.

Sadie felt a similar relief with Kat close and no present danger at their heels. She tried hard not to think about the deadline. Knowing the moment she would leave didn't make it easier. But in this week, just the two of them, she felt more alive than she had in a long time. She felt warm again, sharing her home with Kat, waking to her only to fall asleep alongside her at the end of their day. And everything in between. The pain from her slowly healing ribs hardly mattered. Staying cooped up in her tiny apartment hardly mattered. She couldn't help it. Despite all her reservations. Despite all the reservations, she could tell Kat still felt and somehow set aside for the sake of this week. They still never discussed the easy intimacy they had found themselves wrapped up in. Just continued seamlessly, one day into the other, firmly attached while they set the world aside. The only word Sadie could think of was bittersweet. Bittersweet touches. Bittersweet kisses. Every moment ticking by becoming all the more precious. Holding on tighter and tighter, afraid everything will slip away. But Kat had promised, and she had promised. And as far as she knew she'd never broken a promise to Kat. Not once in her life. She had spent the week with a familiar ache. Not from her ribs but from her chest, this painful urge to tell Kat all the ways she felt. Instead, she waited as the days passed.

The day came for Kat's flight and together they took a taxi to the airport, though Kat had protested saying Sadie didn't need to go all that way just to see her off. Sadie told her there was nothing else she'd rather do. Kat had held her hand every second of the long ride to the airport, pressed against her in the backseat of the cab. It broke Sadie's heart. She wanted to ask if Kat would call her when she landed but couldn't bear to ask.

Kat had promised and that promise would take shape however it would. She willed herself so deeply to trust this beautiful stranger, this long lost friend. Quietly Sadie prayed for traffic, for delayed and canceled flights. For one more moment. One more chance.

The airport came looming in the distance.

When the taxi stopped outside the terminal they both lingered helplessly, too afraid to get out. With a deep breath, Kat reached for the door, her other hand still interlaced with Sadie's. She stepped out of the car, Sadie following closely behind her. With her luggage at her side and Sadie's hand in hers, they stood, neither wanting to part ways.

"I know everything's been tense but…it was really good seeing you again." Sadie squeezed Kat's hand. Kat collected her in her arms careful to avoid hurting Sadie.

"It was long overdue." Kat's voice was hardly a whisper above the din of the airport terminal but Sadie felt the warmth of her breath, the gentleness of her touch and knew everything she meant. "Thank you, Sadie. For everything." Then Kat kissed her and Sadie felt her heart breaking again. She couldn't help the errant tear or the desperate grasp she had on Kat.

"I'm gonna miss you," Sadie answered.

"I won't be far," Kat said.

"Only the other side of the country." Sadie shook her head.

"Just a phone call away." Kat smiled softly, wiping away the fallen tear. "Don't be scared."

Sadie laughed. "Okay."

Kat stroked her cheek. "I have to go." Sadie kissed her once more.

"I know." Reluctantly, Sadie let Kat go. "Have a safe trip." She smiled softly.

"I'm gonna miss you so much," Kat said, kissing Sadie again. Unable to help it despite the stares they were drawing. "I'm not gonna say goodbye because that would be too hard." Sadie nodded and let out a sad laugh. "Until next time?"

"Until next time," Sadie repeated, still holding Kat's hand. Kat grasped her luggage and with a final look and one more kiss on the cheek Kat let her go, disappearing through the sliding airport doors.

For a long while, Sadie stood next to the taxi, the meter still running as she watched Kat through the large glass windows. Heart still breaking as she watched her moving further and further away. Wishing desperately for something to change, for one moment more. Kat turned around locking eyes with Sadie from across the airport, eyes red rimmed and teary. Without further thought, they both moved across the space drawn to one another. They met through the crowd embracing once more. Sadie's arms wrapping around Kat, grounding her.

"It's okay," Sadie whispered. "I promise."

Kat sighed deeply, kissing Sadie fiercely. "No matter what happens. It's okay. I love you so much." And with one more kiss Kat slipped from her arms disappearing through the security gate. Wanting to cry, forcing herself not to, Sadie found a bench and sat, figuring the cab long gone by now. She didn't know what to do but focus on her breathing. In and out. In then out. She felt a vibration in her pocket and remembered her phone. Taking the device out she saw a message illuminate the screen.

"I'll call you as soon as I land," Kat. The phone shook again in Sadie's grasp. "Promise."

Sadie Park will return in Daedalus Detectives: A Hollywood Story

About the Author

S.A. Mossman is a writer and filmmaker. She lives in Los Angeles, California with her partner and their pets. You can find more of her work at saramossman.com

You can connect with me on:
- https://www.saramossman.com
- https://www.twitter.com/SMossman

Also by S.A. Mossman

Last Night At The Fremont

American Despair